TWISTED DEVIL

QUENTIN SECURITY SERIES #1

MORGAN JAMES

CHAPTER
ONE

JASON

The scent of coffee grounds permeated the air, and just the thought of caffeine had my body tingling with anticipation. Unfortunately, I wasn't the only person who needed the shot of adrenaline this morning, and a line of people filled the small shop ahead of me.

I glanced at my phone and let out a little sigh. Goddamn. It was only a little after eleven o'clock, but I felt like I'd been up forever already. Although, with several active cases, I wasn't getting a whole lot of sleep these days, anyway. I needed all the help I could get staying awake, hence my trip to the coffee shop. Though I'd had a cup first thing this morning after working out, I needed the jolt of energy.

I didn't make it to this side of town very often, but we were wrapping up a case a couple of blocks over and the Starbucks across the street had been closed so they could fix a broken pipe. A quick Google search had listed this place, and it was better than nothing.

I mentally went over my list of things to do today,

responding to emails as the line in front of me dwindled. Finally, I stepped up to the counter, ready to order. But the sight that greeted me halted me in my tracks.

A pair of eyes the color of the sky on a cloudless day peered up at me. Framed by sensually long lashes, I felt my words dry up on my tongue as I tumbled headlong into them. They were the brightest blue I'd ever encountered, filled with a sparkling intelligence, and I felt myself drowning in the depths.

"What can I get for you?"

Embarrassment of being caught staring at her washed over me, and my shoulders tightened at the sensation. Christ. What the hell was wrong with me? I cleared my throat. "Just a large coffee, please. Black, no sugar."

"Sure thing." She tapped the screen a couple of times, then smiled up at me, revealing a row of bright white teeth. The way it lit up her face, making those cerulean eyes glow, was like a punch to the solar plexus. "That'll be $4.27, please."

I handed over my credit card, studying her efficient movements as she swiped it through the machine, then handed it back to me. While she waited for my receipt to print, she poured my coffee into a travel cup. "Haven't seen you here before."

"Uh... No." Her statement caught me off guard. "This is my first time."

She smiled and passed me the cup. "I thought so. We're kind of off the beaten path, so we get mostly regulars."

A smattering of freckles, so light I'd missed them before, covered the bridge of her nose and the tops of her cheeks. Her blonde hair was pulled back, highlighting her heart-shaped face and full, sensuous lips. They looked soft and sweet, and I wondered how they'd taste beneath my own.

Would it be too forward to ask her out? Probably. She was

a little on the young side, maybe in her early twenties or so, but I wasn't quite thirty yet.

Jesus. I was already trying to justify asking her out, and I'd only just met her. I couldn't explain exactly why, but I felt a draw to her. She was beautiful, and she caught my attention in a way no other woman ever had. I wanted to see her again—wanted to see if this feeling still existed, that it wasn't some one-time occurrence that would fizzle out as quickly as it'd come.

I was acutely aware of the line of people behind me as she printed off the receipt and handed it to me. "Maybe I'll stop by tomorrow." I almost cringed at the desperate quality my voice held. *Fucking smooth, Jason. Seriously.* "You know, if I'm still in the area."

Those big blue eyes stared up at me. "Then maybe I'll see you tomorrow, stranger."

"Jason." I held her gaze, unable to make myself leave just yet.

A bashful smile curled her lips, and her cheeks flared light pink. There was no maybe about it. I knew I would be back tomorrow.

CHAPTER
TWO

CHLOE

The pungent scent of used coffee grounds rose into the air as I cleaned the machine and got ready to close up for the night. Behind me, Sara helped the final customer cash out, then locked up behind him.

She joined me along the back bar with a little groan. "God, I feel like this was the longest day ever."

I offered a little smile. "I know. My feet are killing me." I shifted on the anti-fatigue mats that lined the floor behind the bar. "I'm just ready to go home and crawl into bed."

"Me too. Are you ready for finals?"

I rolled my eyes as I wiped down the machine. "Hardly. Whitaker is brutal."

"I know, right?" Sara commiserated. "I'm so over it already. I can't wait to be done."

Thank God, I only had a couple more weeks before I was free. Sara and I were in the same microbiology class, and the stodgy old professor was a giant pain in the ass. "I'll be so glad when this semester is over."

"Have you found an internship yet?"

I shook my head. "I've put in some applications, but I haven't heard anything back yet."

"Me either."

The directors at the school were supposed to help with job placement, but so far with the job market the way it was, it was extremely competitive.

"I'll probably have to move out of state," Sara lamented.

Honestly, that didn't sound like the worst idea to me. "Do what you have to do, right?" I shrugged.

"I know, but then I've got Ryan to think about..."

Sara trailed off, and I threw a look her way. "How are you guys doing?"

She rested one hand on the counter and turned to me. "I don't honestly know. Sometimes I think we're great, then other times he pisses me off and I wonder why we're together. I swear, if he wasn't so damn good in bed..."

I knew exactly how she felt. I'd had an on-again, off-again relationship with my boyfriend for nearly two years before I finally broke it off for good a few months ago. I loved Aaron, but we made better friends than a couple. I hadn't dated anyone seriously since then, always too busy with work or school to devote any real time to a relationship.

I thought of the man who'd come in yesterday morning. Jason. I was a little disappointed he hadn't been back to the coffee shop since. It was irrational, I knew, considering we'd talked for a whole two minutes while I poured his coffee. But I'd sworn there was some kind of spark there, and he'd hinted that he would come back. But he hadn't.

I tuned back in to my conversation with Sara. "I think every couple goes through that phase. But if things are meant to work out between you two, they will. Don't decline an amazing job offer on the off chance that you and Ryan stay here and live happily ever after."

Her mouth twisted. "Why is this so hard?"

I cracked a smile. "Adulting sucks, doesn't it?"

"No kidding." She let out a little laugh at the same time her phone dinged with an incoming message. "Speak of the devil," she said.

I watched her fingers fly over the keyboard as she responded. "Why don't you take off?" I suggested. "I can handle the rest."

Sara's eyes flicked to me. "Are you sure? I hate to leave you here by yourself."

"It's no big deal." I waved off her concern. "We're pretty much good anyway. I'll get the dining room cleaned up a bit, then head out."

"If you don't mind..." Sara made puppy dog eyes at me, and I couldn't help but laugh.

"Just go already."

"You're the best." She bounced happily on her toes before grabbing her purse from under the counter and throwing a wave over her shoulder as she left. "See you in the morning!"

I waved as she cut across the parking lot to her small silver sedan, then locked the door once more. I straightened chairs and wiped down tables as I made my way around the small dining area. Once I put all the cleaning materials to rights, I locked up the cash register and turned off the lights. As a safety precaution, the morning crew would handle the bank deposit, so I left the slip on the counter for tomorrow's employees.

I left through the front door, throwing a quick glance around before locking up and heading to my car. Employees had to park on the side to leave room for patrons to park right in front of the shop, so I headed in that direction. As I rounded the corner of the building, a large figure stepped out of the shadows. My breath suspended in my lungs, and my muscles went completely rigid before my brain sent out the signal to run.

Just as I started to turn and bolt away, the man's arms came around my torso. I kicked frantically, my arms pinned at my sides where he held them tightly. Unable to form words, a series of low grunts left my throat as I thrashed against his hold. Finally, I opened my mouth to scream, hoping it would draw attention. As if he knew what I intended, the man's forearm moved up and constricted around my neck.

He leaned back, forcing my back to arch, and the motion put strain on my throat. Black spots danced before my eyes as I struggled to draw in a breath. Two seconds passed, then three. My lungs felt tight, like they were burning, and the man tightened his hold a fraction. The blackness around the edges of my vision slowly bled inward, and I lost the fight to stay awake as my body went limp.

CHAPTER
THREE

JASON

A sick sensation twisted my stomach into knots as I stared at the coffee shop. To think I had just been here two days ago. Now she was missing, apparently abducted after her shift last night.

I glanced at the other agents and policemen standing in the parking lot in front of the coffee shop. "What are you thinking?"

"Never made it to her car," one officer said. "It's still locked, and her purse and keys were found on the sidewalk this morning by the manager."

The local police had called us in first thing this morning as soon as Chloe Danvers had been reported missing. Normally they would have waited since she was of legal age, but considering the circumstances they weren't taking any chances and were treating it as an abduction.

Like the previous three victims, Chloe had blonde hair and bright blue eyes. Three months ago, Kelly Greene was the first woman to disappear from the Chicago area. Her boyfriend had reported her missing when she didn't come home after work. A month later, Jacqueline Howard went missing. The young nursing student lived alone, and she hadn't shown up for her shift at work. After a couple of days, the authorities found her house empty. They still weren't entirely sure when she had been abducted or from where. The third, Caroline Alsept, disappeared last month, reported missing by her parents when she didn't come home. No one had seen them since.

When the locals got the call about Chloe, they had immediately assumed the worst. It appeared that whomever was targeting these young women had crossed state lines, elevating the case from state to federal level. That's where we came in. There were enough similarities between the victims to believe that it could very well be the same person who'd taken them. Speculation had been flying around all morning, everyone trying to guess who the man could be and what had happened to the women.

Chloe's car sat at almost a 90° angle from the front door, and unfortunately, none of the cameras pointed in that direction. I glanced around, then gestured to a small ballet studio across the narrow alley. "Anyone check with them yet?"

"They just opened," replied the detective from the local precinct.

I nodded to my partner. "Let's go check it out."

I scanned the façade of the building as we crossed the street, and I winced internally when I saw no evidence of a camera mounted outside. A little bell over the door jingled as we stepped into the lobbys, and a middle-aged woman greeted us with a smile.

"Can I help you, gentlemen?"

I nodded to her. "I'm Agent Jason Doyle from the FBI," I said, flashing my badge. "This is Agent Sean Kennedy."

Her brows drew slightly together in question. "Nice to meet you, I'm Mary. What can I do for you?"

"Would you happen to have any cameras that overlook that parking lot?" I asked as I pointed toward the coffee shop.

She gestured to a camera positioned over the counter. "I have this one, but it's mostly just to keep an eye on the door. I don't know if you'll be able to see much."

"Anything you have may help." I briefly explained to her what had happened last night. As I spoke of Chloe's disappearance, a lump formed in my throat. God, I still couldn't believe it. Even though I didn't know her all that well, I'd met her—she was real, and it made the case that much more personal. I shoved the thought to the back of my mind and forced my emotions back in check. "Would you mind if we take a look?"

"Not at all."

"Thanks, Mary." She stepped out of the way as we rounded the counter. "Is this the recording from last night?"

She nodded. "It keeps about a week's worth of footage before it starts recording over it."

I was familiar with the system, so I rewound to last night around 8:00 PM when the coffee shop closed. The black and white image on the screen was grainy, but the angle through the large bay window was surprisingly good. I watched on the screen as a young woman left in a small sedan. The minutes ticked away until I finally watched Chloe Danvers exit the coffee shop. As she approached the corner of the building, a lumbering shadow moved in front of her.

I watched as she struggled against his hold until she went limp. The man dragged her backwards so she was off screen, and anticipation raced through my veins. A minute later, a light-colored van drove down the alley that separated the ballet studio from the coffee shop. A street light illuminated the passenger side window, highlighting the man's profile, and I caught a glimpse of the man who had abducted Chloe. He wore a ball cap, but with the light behind him, it was too dark to see his features.

"There's our guy," I murmured. "Now, let's figure out who the hell he is."

I rewound the tape to about 7:00, watching intently for the van. It never came.

"Wonder if he came in from another direction," Kennedy mused.

It was entirely possible. I threw a glance at Mary. "I'd like to review this a little closer."

"Whatever you need," she agreed readily. "I hope you find something."

As I took the disc, thoughts swirled through my mind. We were already sixteen hours behind whoever had taken Chloe. The seconds were rapidly ticking away, and I could only hope we would find her before it was too late.

CHAPTER
FOUR

CHLOE

I came to slowly, and I grimaced as I blinked my eyes open. My body felt cold, and I curled my arms tighter to my chest as goosebumps raced over my skin.

The lighting was dim, and I strained my eyes to see my surroundings. A single bulb hung overhead, just enough to chase away the oppressiveness of the room while still managing to cast a menacing glow over its meager contents.

I shifted slightly, and an answering groan met my ears as the ancient springs of the mattress I lay on squeaked under the movement. Every muscle protested as I pressed my hands flat and pushed to a sitting position.

The room was cold and dank, and the smell of mildew lilted on the air. I took in a gray stone wall, stained dark with age. It reminded me of my grandparents' basement, the wide old stone from the turn of the century—and not the most recent one. Wherever I was, this place was probably at least a hundred years old, judging from the packed dirt floor.

I swallowed hard, then wished I hadn't. My throat ached,

and I rubbed one hand gently along the base. It felt slightly bruised, but most of the damage seemed to be confined to the inside. Which meant no screaming for help. I almost snorted at that. Like anyone would be able to hear me anyway.

I remembered clearly the man coming out of the shadows and snatching me from the sidewalk. After that, everything was a blank slate. I didn't remember seeing his face, and I don't think I ever heard him speak. There was no memory of the trip here, only him choking me until everything went black, then waking up in the cold room.

I gingerly stood and stared down at the mattress. Even in the dim light it appeared filthy, stained with dirt and... Was that blood? Bile rose in my throat and I fought the urge to gag. I shook off the revulsion and quickly averted my eyes, taking in the rest of my surroundings.

In the corner, just a few feet from the revolting mattress, sat a plastic bucket. It was the kind that home-improvement stores sold for odd jobs, and I had a sick feeling I knew exactly what it was for. Like everything else, it was splattered with dirt, the handle missing. That was a shame. I was sure my abductor had thought ahead and removed it so it couldn't be used as a weapon or a tool of some sort.

I was vaguely surprised that whoever had captured me hadn't tied me up or at least bound my hands. That was more than a little unsettling, because that meant the person was positive I wouldn't be able to escape. That only served to strengthen my resolve and find a way out of this Godforsaken place. I was barefoot, though, and I didn't see any signs of my shoes in the immediate surrounding area. I assumed the man had taken them, and it would definitely be a hindrance not having shoes to run in. I didn't care. I would do whatever the hell I had to do to get out of here.

Directly across from me, a solid steel door was situated in the middle of the stone wall. While the rest of the cellar appeared to be ancient, the door looked almost new. Which meant it would be strong, impossible to break. I knew it couldn't be that easy, but I had to check. Cautiously, I approached the door, wondering if someone waited on the other side. Keeping my body positioned to the side so I wouldn't get hit by the door if it swung open, I gingerly touched the handle, testing to see if it was locked. It was.

My heart dropped though I hadn't expected any different. I pressed my ear to the steel and held my breath. Nothing came from the other side. I wasn't sure how thick the door was, but if I couldn't hear anything from the outside, then no one would be able to hear me in here. It was a setback, but I truly expected no less. The man had clearly considered every angle, and the thought sent fear streaming through my veins.

I padded away from the door and began to make a slow circuit of the dim room. As I moved farther away from the single bulb over the mattress, it became harder and harder to see. I kept one hand on the stone wall for guidance as I waited for my eyes to adjust. I moved slowly, putting one foot in front of the other, gradually working my way toward the opposite end of the room.

There was almost no light to speak of except from a dingy window so coated with dirt that I almost missed it at first. It was so high that my fingertips barely brushed the sill. Even if I could get my body up there, I doubted my shoulders could fit in the small rectangular space. Either way, I wouldn't know until I tried.

Placing my hands on the lip of the sill, I braced one foot against the stone wall. It was uneven, which was actually advantageous, and I curled my toes around the top of the stone for balance. I pulled my body up so my chin peeked over the sill. My arm and core muscles shook as I fought to hold myself up. Maneuvering myself as best I could, I braced myself against the wall and ran one hand around the inner edge of the window.

My fingers hit a bump, and I traced the small object. Smooth and cool, the top was flat where it stuck out of the frame at a slight angle. A screw. The window had been screwed shut. I swore softly, not ready to give up yet. My muscles ached, shaking under the strain. The window was narrower than I thought, and even if I tried to break it, I doubted I could fit through the opening.

I readjusted my stance, and my fingers hit a rough patch of stone. I ran my nails along it and found a tiny crevice. I dropped down from the window and shook out my arms. After I'd rested for a second, I reached back up, fumbling blindly at the spot. It felt like a piece of stone had cracked and come loose, and I picked at it until it finally came free.

I turned it over in my hands, feeling along the sharp edges. Thinking it might come in handy later, I held onto it then continued around the room, ending back at the stained mattress where I'd started. Now that I could see the piece of stone a little better, I held it up to the light and inspected it. Closer up, it appeared to be a sliver of mortar that had once held the old stones together. One side was a sharp point, and it widened slightly at the opposite end.

An idea began to brew in the back of my mind and I glanced between the mortar and the mattress. One way or the other, I was getting the hell out of here.

CHAPTER
FIVE

JASON

Several hours later, we had a photo of the captor in hand. Kennedy and I headed back into the coffee shop once more to review their system. Now that we had an idea of who we were looking for, I wanted to see if the man had been in the shop earlier that day.

The manager gave us permission to view the files, and we began yesterday morning as soon as the shop opened. It was a painstakingly long process, scouring the footage for the man in the ball cap. He never showed.

I was frustrated but not surprised. As careful as he seemed to be, it would have been stupid for him to show his face inside. Still, I wanted to check with the workers. One never knew how psychopaths' minds worked. If it was the same guy, he'd clearly gotten away with it several times already. The longer he continued, the cockier he would become—and hopefully he would slip up.

The young woman who'd been working with Chloe last night was here again today, and I wanted to check with her first. "Do you remember anyone out of the ordinary here yesterday? Anyone who stood out?"

She glanced at the screen and shook her head. "Not that I can remember, no."

I showed Sara the photograph. "Does this man seem at all familiar?"

"Do you think...?" Her teeth cut into her bottom lip. "Oh God, I never thought..."

"It's okay," I reassured her.

The young woman's eyes filled with tears. "I never should have left her. I should've stayed so we could walk out together."

"You didn't know this was going to happen," Kennedy soothed her. "In the meantime, though, it might be better to stick together at all times."

She nodded and swiped at the tears sliding down her cheeks. I met Kennedy's gaze and tipped my head to one side, letting him know to join me outside when he was done. I stepped out the front door and glanced around the parking lot and surrounding area again, trying to see it through fresh eyes. At the moment, we only had the footage from the coffee shop and the ballet studio across the street. It would take a while to get a warrant to search the other camera systems from the local businesses.

I fucking hated red tape. Why couldn't people just cooperate? The guy had avoided the cameras all around the coffee shop, solidifying my theory that he had staked it out before making his move. Whoever this guy was, he was smart. He researched. Took his time. He'd gotten away with it before, and he would get away with it again unless we stopped him. What was his weakness?

I propped my hands on my hips and glanced around. A group of women milled around a corner a few blocks west, and I stared at them for a moment, my mind whirling. I tried to put myself in the man's shoes. What would I have done?

He would have stayed far enough away so as to not draw attention to himself, yet close enough that he could see Chloe when she left the coffee shop. It was pure luck for him that Sara had headed out earlier than expected. The man had probably parked down the street so he could fall in behind her when she pulled out of the parking lot. It was pure speculation, but it was all I had to go on at the moment, and I couldn't afford to leave any stone unturned.

I threw a quick look over my shoulder and met Kennedy's gaze as he stepped outside. "Walk with me."

I tipped my head toward the prostitutes, and he fell in beside me. His eyes lit with understanding when he saw where we were headed. "Wonder why the locals didn't question them already?"

"Probably weren't out this morning."

Several pairs of wary eyes turned toward us as we approached, and I lifted one hand in a little wave to staunch their concern. A young woman in a candy-red leather brassiere sidled toward me on sky-high heels. "What can I do for you, sugar?"

"Were you by chance working last night?"

Her head tipped slightly to one side. "Depends who's asking."

I pulled my wallet from my back pocket, then dug out a twenty and passed it to her. Without even glancing at it, she tucked it into the cup of her bra and nodded for me to continue my line of questioning. "A man came through here last night in a light-colored van. Would you happen to remember anything about the driver?"

A little smirk tipped her lips. "Honey, I see a lot of cars come through here on any given night."

Kennedy held up the grainy black-and-white photograph

we pulled from the ballet studio. "A young woman was abducted from the coffee shop down the street last night."

I pointed toward the corner. "I have a feeling he may have been parked down this way somewhere. I want to make sure we find this guy and keep you ladies safe."

A battle brewed in her eyes for a moment before she glanced over her shoulder. "Renee."

At the sound of her name, a young brunette ambled forward. "Yeah?"

The first girl pointed at the picture Kennedy held. "You remember this guy last night?"

Renee nodded. "Parked right up there." She pointed about a block over. "Thought he might be looking for some fun for the night, so I spoke to him. Asshole was rude. Told me to leave him the hell alone."

"Do you remember what he looked like?"

Renee shook her head. "He was the forgettable type. Couldn't really see all of his features anyway with the hat on."

Damn. I tamped down my disappointment. "Well, thank you anyway."

Kennedy and I turned to leave but were brought up short by the woman's voice. "Hey."

I threw a quick look at her. She pulled out her phone and took a second to flip through it before holding it up to me. "I took a picture of the van."

My heart rate jacked up as I took the phone. "He kind of creeped me out," she said. "You never can tell with people."

"No, you can't," I agreed. I enlarged the photo on the screen, and a sense of satisfaction welled up inside me. "Got you, you son of a bitch."

CHAPTER
SIX

CHLOE

I stared down at the twin-sized mattress that had housed God knew how many women before me. Sliding my fingers underneath, I awkwardly maneuvered it so it was upside down. The bottom was just as disgusting as the top, and I grimaced. I picked up the sliver of mortar and moved to the top right corner of the mattress.

Digging the sharp end into the fabric, I wiggled it back and forth until it cut a tiny hole in the material. Excitement surged through my blood, and I dragged the mortar downward, using sawing motions to cut away at it. Once I had a tear about a foot long, I turned at a right angle and continued to cut until I had a large rectangular piece of cloth. I tore a smaller strip off, about an inch wide, then tied it around the base of the mortar sliver.

I kept adding layers until the cloth handle was easier to hold and wield. When I was done, I flipped the mattress over to conceal the missing fabric, then stood and grabbed up the mortar. It would serve as a makeshift shank in case the man came back, but I had other plans for it at the moment.

Readjusting my grip on the mortar, I crossed to the door. There was no window, just a single slab of steel that probably weighed close to a hundred pounds. But that wasn't the important part. What mattered was that the door swung inward, so the hinges were on my side.

I examined them, studying the way the pins secured the door in place. The pins were about four inches long, and there was one at the top, middle, and bottom of the door. If I could work those free, I could potentially move the door and escape. I didn't delude myself into thinking that it would be an easy task. But it was my only option at the moment, and I refused to just sit here and wait for the man to come back.

Staring at the door, I decided that the top pin was going to be the hardest. Even standing next to it, the pin was still several inches above my head. The head of the pin was flat, but there was a tiny space between the head and where it rested on the hinge. I wedged the sharp end of the sliver under the head and wiggled. Nothing. I tried again, but it refused to move. I let out a frustrated sigh and shook my head. Damn it! This had to work.

I repositioned the sliver, angling it upward and bumping it with the heel of my hand. My heart jumped in my chest as the pin slid upward. It was no more than a millimeter, but it was better than nothing. I kept going for what felt like forever. The pin was wedged tightly in there, and it was stiff with disuse. My shoulders and upper back screamed from the effort of constantly holding my arms over my head.

After what had to be more than an hour, the pin was only halfway extracted from its hole but I didn't dare let go. I refused to sacrifice the progress I'd made. My muscles burned with exhaustion and every nerve ending felt like it was on fire. My hand was stiff, and blood dripped down my fingers where my nails had broken and my skin had been torn ragged from picking at the pin on the door. It was fight for freedom or die down here. Said that way, it was really no choice.

Resolve strengthened, I forced myself to continue. With each minute that passed, the pin moved closer and closer to the top of the hinge, and my hope grew. I wiggled it back and forth, working it upward, and I nearly cried with relief when it finally popped free.

I glanced at the pin in my hand. It was such a tiny thing, yet could very well be the deciding factor between life and death.

Every part of me was physically and mentally exhausted, and I took a moment to relax. Just to be on the safe side, I trudged back to the mattress and stowed the pin, along with the tiny sliver of mortar, underneath. Although I had put it off as long as possible, I could no longer ignore my body's pressing needs. I threw a look of disdain at the bucket in the corner. I relieved myself, then placed it far away from the bed.

I had just gotten back to the mattress when a thump from the direction of the door made my heart jump in my chest. A metallic click echoed in the room a second before the door swung open.

Fear rose up, threatening to choke me as a large, dark figure filled the doorway. Backlit from behind, all I could see was the bulk of his huge body. Without meaning to, I cowered in fear, shrinking away from him until my back hit the hard wall behind me. I pressed my hands to the cool stone, fighting to stay upright.

The man stepped into the room, then closed and re-locked the door behind him using a key. My heart sank as he slipped the key into his pocket then slowly approached. I flicked a quick glance at the mattress. The mortar was underneath, along with the door pin.

Did I risk going for it? As a weapon it would be fairly

useless unless the door was open, or I had access to the key. The likelihood of me incapacitating him enough to get the key in his pocket was slim to none. I hated feeling helpless, but I was going to have to let this play out for the time being.

His heavy footsteps echoed in my ears, and my pulse increased with every inch he drew closer. My lungs constricted and every muscle trembled as he stepped into the light. The dark shadows outlined his craggy face in stark relief, making him look even more imposing. Those soulless brown eyes pinned me in place, and I felt frozen, unable to think, unable to move—unable to do anything but drag shallow breaths into my lungs, tight with fear.

He stared at me for what felt like forever before he finally spoke. "Strip."

Combined with the gravelly voice, it took a few seconds for the word to register in my brain. "W-what?"

"Strip!" he thundered, his words bouncing off the walls.

Panic ricocheted through me, and I shook my head. "Please don't do this, I—"

He took another menacing step forward. Beside his leg, his hand flicked forward and a long blade appeared, glinting in the dim light.

"Oh, God, please..."

I clenched my hands into fists as he grabbed my shirt and sank the knife into the fabric, splitting it easily from collar to hem. I shook like a leaf, my mind spinning as I fought to come up with a way to escape. "I... I'll do it."

He studied me for a second, then finally nodded. Bile rose up my throat at the thought of exposing myself to him. The blood on the mattress caught my eye and I fought back the tears clogging my throat. I had to find a way out of this. If I could just get him to leave, even for awhile, I might have a chance at getting the door open.

I shrugged out of my ruined shirt and dropped it to the

ground next to the mattress. He watched intently as I moved to my pants next, pushing them down until I was in just my bra and underwear.

I glanced up at him, and he jerked his head. "On the bed."

My stomach twisted with a combination of revulsion and fear. If I followed his directions, he would rape me or worse. "I—"

His hand shot out, grabbing my biceps and hauling me against him. I gasped, and the stench of his body hit my nostrils. Coupled with the feel of him against me, I fought the urge to gag. "P-please…"

My feet skimmed the floor as he lifted me bodily and practically slammed me onto the mattress. The motion sucked the air from my lungs, momentarily stunning me. Before I could react, he was between my legs, his hands on me. Fear choked me as he gripped the strap of my bra then jerked it down, exposing me to his view.

He roughly palmed my breast, and I bit my tongue to keep from crying out. He held me in place with one hand on my shoulder, while the other moved south. He cupped my mound outside my panties, and tears burned my eyes. Oh, God…. I couldn't let him do this.

I flailed my left hand toward the edge of the mattress, but my range of motion was limited. There was no way I could get to the mortar or the pin to stab him. I had no leverage with him between my thighs, so I was going to have to outsmart him. His mouth dipped and he captured my nipple in a slobbery kiss that turned my stomach inside out.

In one last-ditch effort, I begged again, trying the only thing I could think of to turn him off. "Please don't do this. Not now. I... I'm on my period."

The man halted, his hand hovering just over my underwear, those sinister eyes staring down at me. I forced myself to stay strong, to not cower under his gaze. "Show me."

My mouth dropped open a little bit. "What?"

"Show me," he repeated.

Oh, God. He was testing me, just waiting for me to fail. What if he found out I'd lied to him? Still trembling, I dipped my hand beneath the waistband of my underwear and brushed my center. I slowly withdrew it and, keeping my hand in the shadow created by his huge body, held my fingers up to him. They were ragged and torn from picking at the pin on the door, and I prayed that he wouldn't be able to see the blood had already dried and begun to flake off. He hesitated so long I thought for sure he would call my bluff.

Suddenly, his weight lifted away as he clambered off the mattress. Without another word, he snatched up my clothes, spun on a heel and strode toward the door. I watched as he unlocked it, then slammed and re-locked it behind him.

Silence fell in his absence and it was somehow both the most welcome and most intimidating sound I'd ever heard in my life. I wasn't sure how long I lay there before relief welled up and I let out a sob. That had been too close. I didn't know if I would survive a second time. One thing was certain—he would be back again, and soon.

Moving slowly, I tucked myself back into my bra then, climbing to my hands and knees, I crawled over to the edge of the mattress and fished out the piece of mortar. I didn't have a second to lose.

CHAPTER
SEVEN

JASON

I leaned back in my chair and rubbed my eyes. They burned from staring at the screen for so long, trying to make sense of the barely visible numbers and letters. The back of the van was splattered with mud, and dirt obscured 90% of the license plate. I'd been running a combination of potential numerals but so far had come up empty.

I glanced up as Kennedy approached. "How's it going?"

I pointed to the screen. "Same as it was about an hour ago."

The first digit on the license plate I suspected was either an E or an F. The fourth digit was what I thought looked like a number nine. One of the techs was running all of the license plates with numbers that fell within that particular sequence, but even narrowing it down to white vans, there were still too many options. I had to find something else.

I pushed away from my desk and headed to the kitchenette where I refilled my mug with the coffee that'd been sitting out for hours. The smell of it alone reminded me of Chloe, and my heart twisted. I leaned against the cabinets, stirring my coffee, lost in thought.

Agent Kevin Mazzarra stepped up next to me. "Any leads on your case?"

I sighed and shook my head. "Not yet. What are you guys working on? Still the investment fraud?"

"Yep. Boring as hell." He nodded and pulled the empty Diet Pepsi can from the koozie and tossed it in the recycle bin.

My eyes lit on the logo printed on the insulator, and something sparked in my memory. "I'll catch you later."

"Good luck."

I headed back to my computer and studied the frame until I found what I was looking for. I enlarged the picture, focusing on the back of the van. Mud covered most of it, but what appeared to be several points, like a large sunburst, was situated in the lower left corner just above the bumper.

I waved Kennedy over. "Think this could be a dealership logo?"

He studied the screen, then nodded. "Could be. Too defined to be mud splatter."

"The van, or this plate at least, is registered in Illinois. Let's pull dealerships within a fifty-mile radius and see if any of them have insignias that might look like this."

Soon we had a list of 463 dealerships, both new and used, to sift through. Christ. This was going to take forever. One by one, we pulled them up and crossed them off the list. But on number forty-seven, we hit pay dirt. The five lines that stuck up in a sort of trident were a match to Norton Chevrolet. I picked up the phone and punched in the number for the sales manager.

She answered a few rings later, and I introduced myself. "Ms. Miles, my name is Jason Doyle with the Federal Bureau of Investigation. I'm wondering if you can help me with something."

"I can try," she offered. "What do you need?"

The van itself was a newer model that they had just started producing about five years ago. I relayed to Ms. Miles the model number of the van. "Could you please provide me a list of purchases from the past five years?"

"I should be able to do that," she said slowly. "I'll email you what I find, but I have to warn you, that's a pretty popular model."

"No problem. Anything you can do will be helpful." I gave her my email address then hung up and focused on the screen in front of me, racking my brain for another way to figure out who the hell this guy was.

My thoughts were broken nearly an hour later when my email dinged with an incoming message. I opened it and barely held back a groan as I skimmed the long list of names. At least it was a starting point. I hit the button to print it, then made my way to the printer. I tipped my head toward Kennedy. "Just got the list of purchases from Norton. Want to help me check them off?"

"Sure."

I handed him a couple of pages, then returned to my desk. It felt like hours had passed before Kennedy jumped up. "Hey, I think I've got it."

He passed me the paper with a highlighted name. Jeffrey Wainwright. I tapped the name into the database and held my breath. "Caucasian, 38 years old, brown hair, brown eyes. No priors."

Either this wasn't the guy we were looking for, or he'd been extremely careful up until now. "Let's check his home address," I said as I pulled up the address on file with the DMV.

I pinpointed it on the map and took a look at the surrounding areas. Located northwest of town, the area was fairly isolated. I used my forefinger to draw a little circle on the map. "No homes within a four-mile radius." Which meant no one to run to for help. My gut twisted, and the hairs on the back of my neck lifted.

Kennedy tipped his head. "I think it's a good bet. Let's check it out."

CHAPTER
EIGHT

CHLOE

My fingers ached and sweat dripped into my eyes, but I didn't dare stop. I wasn't sure how long ago the man had left. Hours, probably. I was exhausted, but I refused to sleep.

I had finally gotten the bottom pin removed. All that was left now standing between me and freedom was the middle pin. And whatever lay beyond this room. But I couldn't think about that now. All I could focus on was doing one thing at a time. I needed to get out of here, away from my captor and whatever horrible fate he had in store for me.

Wedging the tip of the mortar between the top of the pin and the hinge, I began to wiggle it. Just like the other two pins, the process was slow and grueling. Millimeter by millimeter it began to lift. I worked at it with my sore, bloodied fingers until it was almost free of the hole.

My heart leapt with excitement as it teetered there in the hinge, just millimeters of cool metal separating me from freedom. Not a full second later, a sound beyond the room stopped me cold.

Thump.

Thump.

Thump.

Oh, God. He was back.

My breath sawed in and out of my lungs as his tread moved closer and closer. I fought the urge to hyperventilate as my pulse kicked up. I had to stay strong; I had to get out of here. After he came in last time, I knew I didn't have a choice —next time he would rape me or worse.

I clutched the mortar as tightly as I could with my damaged fingers and stood off to the side. The sound of the lock disengaging seemed magnified in the empty room, and I watched in a sort of slow motion as the door swung inward. With only the middle pin barely holding it up, the door wobbled in its frame.

"What the...?"

I took advantage of the man's surprise and shoved the door toward him as hard as possible. The remaining pin popped out of its place, dislodging the door. The heavy slab of steel toppled from its frame, and the man let out a terse curse as it smashed into him.

I didn't waste another second. I bolted through the opening, following the dim light beyond to a narrow set of stone steps that led up to what I assumed was the house. Ignoring the man swearing a blue streak behind me, I sprinted up the stairs as fast as my feet could carry me.

I paused only briefly on the landing, casting a quick look around. It took a second for my eyes to register what they were seeing. Huge wooden beams stretched high overhead, and a labyrinth of wooden stalls lay in front of me. I was wrong; it wasn't a house. It was a barn.

The man's footsteps pounded on the stairs behind me, and I knew I didn't have much time. I darted forward, frantically searching for a door. Where the hell was it? The light was dim inside the huge barn, and everything seemed to be made of wood. I couldn't differentiate one wall from another. I spun in place, looking for any avenue of escape. My eyes connected with a ray of sunlight spilling in through a dusty window, and I lunged toward it.

As I neared it, I realized the window was located inside an old stall. I threw the rickety door wide in my haste to get to it, and my feet slipped on the hay-covered floor as I rounded the corner. Pain radiated upward through my body as my hip slammed into the post, but I shoved it down and scrambled to right myself.

Spying an old bucket lying on the ground I scooped it up, then swung as hard as I could, aiming for the window. It sailed through the delicate glass, and the window shattered with a satisfying crash. The bucket made a loud clang as it landed on the grass below amidst the shards of glass just as a loud growl sounded behind me. I placed my hands on the windowsill, ignoring the bite of pain as the glass cut into my palms. The man's fingers grabbed at me, but I evaded his grasp and launched myself through the opening.

Agony ripped through me as I landed sideways on the hard ground, but I forced myself to keep going. Dredging up every ounce of will I possessed, I staggered to my feet and ran as fast as I could. I dared a single glance behind me just in time to see the man's angry face outlined in the window.

It was a mistake.

I never should have looked behind me. Because in the next second, a pair of strong arms wrapped around me, stealing my breath and stopping my heart.

CHAPTER
NINE

JASON

Chloe's tiny body slammed into me, and I let out a small oomph of surprise as I wrapped my arms around her to steady us both. A shrill scream rent the air, and Chloe exploded into action. Her arms and legs swung wildly, jerky with terror.

"Chloe." I immediately released her, but stayed close. "I'm here to help you, Chloe. I'm with the FBI."

Her arms continued to windmill in my direction, desperately trying to fend me off. She stumbled sideways under the force of her movements, and I shot out one hand to catch her. "You're okay. You're safe, Chloe."

I kept talking to her, kept using her name over and over, hoping it would eventually break through her haze of fear. "I'm not going to hurt you, I promise."

In my peripheral vision, I was dimly aware of my other team members circling the house and barn, trapping the man inside. They would take care of him. Right now, Chloe was my main priority.

If I hadn't known Wainwright was responsible the second

we pulled into the driveway of the rundown old house, the shattering of glass from the ancient barn was a dead giveaway. Watching Chloe tumble through the broken window had nearly stopped my heart.

She was almost completely naked, her slender body clad only in a bra and underwear. Her skin was filthy, and streaks of blood covered her arms and legs. I couldn't begin to decipher how badly she was injured.

All of a sudden, her movement stopped. As if she'd just exerted every ounce of energy, she crumpled to the ground in a heap. I dropped to a knee next to her, speaking in a low voice as I did so. "You're safe now," I assured her. "He can't hurt you anymore."

Her arms covered her face and head as she curled into herself on the dewy grass, and her body trembled violently. "Chloe, do you remember me? My name is Jason. We met at the coffee shop a few days ago. I—"

Before I could blink, she launched herself into me, her arms wrapping around my neck like a vise. Her sobs filled the air, her erratic breathing leaving her mouth in great, gasping pants next to my ear. I pulled her to me, holding her tight as protectiveness washed over me.

"You're okay. You're safe." I gently patted her back as she clung to me.

I watched over her shoulder as my team apprehended Wainwright. His dark gaze was fixed on Chloe wrapped in my arms, and the look on his face was enough to send chills down my spine even from this far away.

"You're so brave, Chloe. I'm so proud of you." I continued to speak to her, offering soothing reassurances until the police and medics showed up. By then, her sobs had quieted and her body relaxed in my arms.

"I need to have the medic check you out," I said to her in a soft voice. "Is that okay?"

Her arms tightened around my neck, and her head moved against my shoulder in what I assumed was a nod. I glanced down at her feet. They were a bloody mess, and the sight sent fury spiking through me. "I'm going to carry you over there, okay?"

Her head bobbed another nod, and I lifted her into my arms as carefully as I could. "They got him, Chloe. Everything will be okay."

She kept her arms linked around my neck, face tucked into my chest, like she couldn't bear to look at the place she'd just escaped. I didn't blame her.

"We'll get you all taken care of," I promised.

The low sound of approaching sirens filled the air, and her tear-stained face slowly lifted from my chest. "Is he gone?"

I glanced over to the police cruiser where Wainwright sat ensconced inside the backseat. "He will be soon."

She pressed her forehead to my chest and shook her head. "I don't want to see him."

"You don't have to," I said fiercely as the ambulance pulled onto the scene. "You just keep your eyes on me. Okay?"

Her head moved against my throat, and a little flicker of regret moved through me as I stepped up next to the medic. They already had the stretcher out and ready to go. They would need to treat all of her wounds and probably get an IV started, judging from the looks of her. I gently lay her down, then stepped back.

"Wait!" Her eyes flew to me, and one arm shot out in my direction. "Don't leave."

"Okay." I started to reach for her hand then stopped, not wanting to hurt her further. I rested my hand on the gurney next to her. "I'm right here. I won't let anything happen to you."

Her chest rose and fell on a deep breath and she gave a little nod. As I climbed into the ambulance behind them, my words reverberated in my mind, and a strange feeling welled up inside me. Protectiveness, but something else. Something stronger. I battled it down, shoving it to the back of my mind.

My gaze fell to her hands resting gently over her abdomen, and my stomach flipped at the sight. Rage simmered in my veins as I took in the raggedly torn nails, the battered, bloody flesh. I swore with every fiber of my being that he would pay for hurting her.

CHAPTER
TEN

CHLOE

I tipped my head back against the mound of pillows and let out a sigh. Ever since I'd been admitted to the hospital yesterday afternoon, it had been a whirlwind of activity. My mom and dad had both stopped in to see me, but that was more exhausting than comforting.

Divorced since I was four, they were the epitome of dysfunctional. Both had remarried, and I had five stepsiblings, none of whom had come to visit me. Not that I minded. That was more than I wanted to deal with at the moment.

My mother was always super dramatic, and somehow she managed to turn every situation around and make it about herself. My father, after making sure I wasn't mortally wounded, had lectured me on the importance of paying closer attention to my surroundings.

A little over a half hour ago, I had feigned sleep and they had both finally left me in blessed silence. I turned my head and stared out the window. I couldn't sleep. Over the past twenty-four hours, I had dozed for probably a total of thirty minutes.

Every time I closed my eyes, I saw him. I could feel his arms coming around me outside the coffee shop, choking off my air. I smelled the dank mildew of the cellar, saw the bloodstained mattress in the corner.

A shiver racked my body and my fingers clenched the thin white blanket that covered the bed. Thank God the police had shown up when they did. Had they arrived even a few minutes later, I likely would've been back in the cellar... Or dead. I wasn't entirely sure which would have been worse.

Two quick knocks came from the door, and my heart jumped into my throat as I snapped my head in that direction. Jason stood outlined in the doorway, looking slightly uneasy. "May I come in?"

I drew in a deep breath to settle my heart. "Of course."

He moved to the chair next to the bed, never tearing his eyes from me. "How are you feeling?"

I lifted one shoulder. "Fine."

"This isn't an interview." He lifted a hand and reached for me. Suspended in midair, just inches away, he froze. I saw his gaze linger on the bandages that had been wrapped around my hands, protecting my damaged fingers. He swallowed hard, his Adam's apple bobbing with the movement.

"It's okay," I said softly.

He shook his head but didn't say anything else for several seconds. He seemed lost in thought, and my stomach twisted with apprehension as I waited for him to break the tense silence.

He looked... furious. Nothing like the man I'd met at the coffee shop several mornings ago. He hadn't even looked like that yesterday when he'd pulled me into his arms to protect me.

My gaze followed his movements as he finally settled his

hand on the bed right next to my forearm. I stared at it, a dozen emotions rocketing through me. Relief that he hadn't touch me. Disappointment for the same reason.

It was irrational, but a huge part of me wanted to feel his skin on mine. I wanted the comfort and compassion. I wanted to feel as safe as I had yesterday when he'd carried me to the ambulance to keep from further damaging my feet.

"Scared," I finally admitted, answering his initial question. "Angry. Disappointed."

"Disappointed?" I could feel Jason studying me as I nodded. "Why are you disappointed?"

"Because." I swallowed hard, the memory of leaving the coffee shop that night pressing in around me. "I should have asked Sara to stay. I never should have left alone. If I had just looked around, been a little more cautious—"

"Don't you dare take the blame for that." Jason's voice brooked no argument. "He made those choices, not you."

I lifted my eyes to his. "I know, but..."

Jason shook his head. "That could have happened to anyone. Hell, it could even happen to me."

I was positive he was just trying to make me feel better, and I let out a little snort. "I seriously doubt that."

"What I'm saying is, it's easy to take advantage of someone when you catch them by surprise. What matters is that you escaped. You stayed strong. You never gave in."

His dark eyes drew me in, and I was helpless to resist. "I couldn't," I whispered. "I knew if I stayed down there I would die. I kept looking at that disgusting mattress and wondering how many times he'd done it before. How many families are out there needing closure?"

Something flashed across Jason's face, and he scooted a fraction closer. "What you did is absolutely incredible. My team is working the scene right now to see if we can answer any of those questions."

"Good. What happens next?" I asked.

He stared at me for a second, gauging my emotional stability. "I'm fine," I assured him. "Knowing what to expect will help."

He gave a little nod. "Right now he's over at County waiting for his arraignment."

"What does that mean?"

Jason blew out a little breath. "Basically what happens is they'll take him to court and ask him to plead either innocent or guilty, then—"

"But he's guilty," I cut in. "You know that. You literally saw me running away from the house." My voice had raised several octaves with hysteria, but I couldn't help it.

"I know," Jason said, "but that's how our justice system works. Everyone is given the benefit of the doubt. It's going to be a long process, and it will most likely get worse before it gets better."

"I don't understand." Tears burned my eyes. "You saw…"

My voice broke, and Jason leaned forward. "I know. And that's exactly why I'm going to do everything in my power to put that fucker away for the rest of his life."

The fierceness in his tone and the promise in his eyes should have scared me. But it didn't. "Okay," I whispered. "I trust you."

Jason's dark gaze swept over my face, searching my eyes before dropping lower. For a split second I thought he was going to kiss me. I watched his shoulders rise and fall on a deep breath before he sat back in his chair, and disappointment slammed into me. It was irrational I knew, but I couldn't help it.

After everything that had happened, I shouldn't want anyone to touch me. And truthfully, I didn't. But this man in front of me was so strong, so trustworthy. I knew I could depend on him. I swore I felt something between us, but I wasn't ready to act on it yet. Everything was still too fresh. I swallowed down my insecurities, shoving them aside to deal with later.

"Thank you... for everything."

An emotion I didn't recognize darkened his eyes. I felt the slight tug of the blankets as his fingers skimmed upward until they settled on my forearm, just above the bandages. I was transfixed by the sight of his skin against mine, the heat and the feel of him. A million emotions rocketed through my body. His fingers were long and strong, and I could feel the slightly hardened edge of the calluses tipping the ends. His touch was both unsettling and extremely comforting.

Jason gave an abbreviated shake of his head, but his hand stayed in place. "I was just doing my job."

Was this part of his job to him? Stopping in to check on victims? The question got stuck on my tongue, and I swallowed it down. I wasn't sure I wanted the answer to that. I remembered the way he held me close after I'd escaped from that hell. He had been gentle and kind, and he hadn't left me until we reached the hospital and my family had arrived.

His fingers had curled into my forearm as he spoke, and I was acutely aware of his touch. Heat seeped into my body, coiling around my heart and warming me from the inside. I wanted to believe I was more than just a job, but I didn't dare ask.

Jason looked as conflicted as I felt. His fingers tightened infinitesimally, then slowly slipped away as he stood. "I should let you get some rest."

"Okay." I nodded, feeling an emptiness spreading through my chest.

I watched as he moved toward the door. Was this the last time I would ever see him? "Jason?"

He turned at the sound of his name, one hand on the door handle, eyes dark and unreadable. "Yeah?"

"Will..." God, how stupid I sounded. My cheeks burned, and I shook my head as I forced a smile. "I just wanted to say thank you... again."

"You're welcome."

It seemed as if time had frozen, and the world slowed to a stop as we stared at each other. Finally, he gave a slow nod. "Once you're feeling better, we'll have some questions for you."

I blinked. Someone from the bureau had already been in to talk with me earlier this morning. I'd told her everything I knew, but...

Jason's face was intent as he stared at me, a secret message in the depths of his eyes. "I'll see you soon, Chloe."

With that, he was gone. I couldn't help the little flutter in my chest as the door closed behind him with a soft click. What did that mean? All I knew was, Jason was a man of his word. He'd promised to see me again, so I knew he would be back.

And for some strange reason, I looked forward to it.

CHAPTER
ELEVEN

JASON

Extension cords weaved together and snaked down the steps to the cellar. Half a dozen work lights had been set up throughout the room, powered by the generator that hummed noisily in the background. The basement had been oppressive before, lit only by the single dim light bulb. But this was worse.

The harsh fluorescent glow highlighted every crack in the ancient stone wall, the damp spots where the water had penetrated the earth, and the old dirt floor. It illuminated the scratch marks its previous residents had carved into the walls, the lines stained dark with blood.

My stomach threatened to heave at the gruesome sight. I didn't want to consider how many women had endured the same fate. How close had Chloe come to being raped and killed by that monster? We had searched every inch of the barn and basement, but as of yet there was no sign of the women, nothing to indicate they were ever here except the blood on the mattress and walls.

The crime scene techs were collecting as much evidence on site as possible so they wouldn't lose anything during transportation. They would take samples of the blood and send it out for DNA testing, but that could take forever. With this case, we had to dot every i and cross every t. I had to make sure that justice would be served for Chloe and every woman who'd preceded her. Every case was important, but seeing her on the receiving end had rattled me. I didn't even know her all that well, but this case had affected me more than usual, and on a much deeper level.

Walking through the barn earlier had turned my stomach. Hooks and old farm implements lined the walls, and they too would be tested for DNA. I could only imagine the kind of damage a person could inflict with those. One of the biggest questions we'd had so far was what Wainwright had done with the victims. If what we suspected was true, at least six women had been held here against their will. There wasn't enough evidence yet to prove he'd killed them—but we'd find it.

I watched as a tech lifted what appeared to be a long blonde hair from the mattress. She bagged it carefully then set it aside and continued her perusal of the basement. The door had been removed from its hinges, and I knew from Chloe's statements that she had been integral in that process. I moved toward the edge of the doorway and examined the hinges where the door would attach. Bile burned a path up my throat when I saw her blood on the hinge.

I couldn't begin to imagine what that was like for her. I couldn't forget the sight of her bloodied and battered hands and feet. I'd frozen earlier in the hospital room. I'd started to reach for her but seeing the thick white bandages wrapped around her hands had stopped me cold. The knowledge of what she'd endured had filled me with a fury so blindingly intense I'd physically had to stop and take a breath.

I almost couldn't reconcile the sweet, sassy barista from

the coffee shop with the woman who lay in the hospital bed. The past few days had changed her. There was a wariness in her eyes, a tension in her face. I wanted so badly to take all that away. I knew it was wrong—but I had to touch her.

She was so brave, so determined, so strong. The idea of her being here made me sick. Not to mention the others. How could someone do something so horrific? I took in the bloodstained mattress with barely restrained rage. She told us that he hadn't raped her, though he tried. She had apparently put him off, and for that I was grateful. She'd endured so much as his captive; he'd stolen her innocence, her trust in people. I was relieved he hadn't managed to take that from her too.

Everything seemed to be well in hand down here, so I headed back up the steps and into the barn. God knew there was plenty of space around here to bury the bodies, but an inspection of the grounds showed no recent disturbance. There were no holes, no piles of freshly turned dirt. The women's bodies had never turned up that we had found, and I had a terrible feeling that they were here somewhere. I just wasn't sure where.

Shelving the thought for the moment, I made my way into the old farmhouse. Everything had been photographed, but people still milled around the scene, looking for any evidence we could find. Linking the DNA in the basement would be helpful, but we needed something more concrete. We needed solid evidence that he'd killed the women so he would go to jail for a very long time.

I met Kennedy inside. "Anything new?"

"Not yet." He shook his head. "If we don't find something..."

He trailed off but I picked up his train of thought. We'd spent the past day and a half scouring the property, but even the cadaver dogs hadn't hit on anything tangible. If we didn't find something soon, we were completely dependent on the DNA. And I was afraid that wouldn't be enough.

"I think I've got something," one of the techs called.

Kennedy and I met him halfway, and he held out a small wooden box. The lid was flipped back, and the items inside glittered in the light. I took in the necklaces, the silver ring, a pair of gold hoop earrings. I pulled up a picture on my phone and compared it to the necklace in the box, the pendant carved into a scripted letter E.

"Looks like Erin Stuart's necklace."

Kennedy nodded. "Trophies."

It was a step in the right direction, but we still needed to find the women. The families needed the closure, and the victims needed to be put to rest. As the tech bagged each piece of jewelry for evidence, Kennedy and I moved outside. I slid my sunglasses into place and scanned the large farm. The lowing of cows in the far pasture met my ears, along with the soft snuffle of the pigs penned up behind the barn.

As soon as we cleared the scene, we would have someone come take the livestock. Something spun in the back of my mind, twisting my stomach. The women's bodies never turned up, so he had to have disposed of them somewhere. I couldn't help but wonder...

I spoke as I walked toward the pig pen. "Have you ever spent much time around pigs?"

Kennedy shook his head. "Nope. Whatcha thinking?"

"Fuckers will eat anything. My uncle had a farm out west, and he'd lectured my brothers and me about the importance of staying away. They would attack humans if they were scared... or hungry."

I remembered watching The Wizard of Oz as a kid and wondering why everyone had freaked out about Dorothy falling into the pen with the pigs. But seeing them rut through their food and destroy everything in sight had answered that question.

A sick feeling curled through my stomach as I regarded the hogs. "See those teeth? They'll cut through just about anything."

Kennedy's face hardened at my implication, then he yelled over his shoulder at the techs. "Can we get someone over here?"

We assembled the team and came up with a plan to remove the hogs and dredge the pen. Though the animals would have obliterated most of the bodies, there had to be something. Hours later, their hard work paid off in the form of a tooth. Only one so far, but it was a start. The knowledge that the women had been here—that Wainwright had disposed of them right where I stood—stoked the fire simmering in my veins. I was going to do everything in my power to make sure justice was served.

Whatever I felt for Chloe, I needed to set it aside. She deserved better, and I couldn't afford to ruin this now. I had to keep my distance—for both of us... No matter how much it hurt.

CHAPTER
TWELVE

CHLOE

I drew in a deep breath and wiped my sweaty palms on my dress pants. Next to me, my attorney laid a gentle hand on my shoulder. "You're going to do great."

I shot her a little smile and tried to shove down the butterflies battering the insides of my stomach.

"Just remember what we practiced," she said. "Ignore him and just tell the jury exactly what happened."

I gave a shaky nod and swallowed hard. I knew the defense attorney would try to trip me up; it was his job. Fortunately, there seemed to be quite a bit of evidence stacked against Jeffrey Wainwright. When they had searched the house, they apparently found jewelry from multiple other victims, along with the remains of six other women. My testimony would help to put the man behind bars, hopefully for life. But first I had to get through it.

Part of me wanted to go in there, look him dead in the eye, and demand he admit everything he'd done. But the other half of me was terrified. Even though nearly a year had passed, I still remembered it like it was yesterday. Wainwright had never made bail, and today's trial would determine whether he was ultimately guilty of the crimes he undoubtedly committed. I hoped the jury would listen to my version of events and charge him accordingly.

"You ready?"

I nodded to Jennifer. "Yeah, I'm good."

"Let's go."

The judge called me to the stand, and I climbed into the small booth where I laid my hand on the Bible and repeated the vow to tell the truth of that day. My heart felt like it was lodged in my throat, and I swallowed hard as I stared out over the sea of faces. I was looking for one in particular, and relief flooded me as Jason's dark eyes stared back at me from halfway across the room.

Though I'd only seen him a handful of times since that day at the hospital, he promised he would be here with me every step of the way. I knew he was incredibly busy, and it meant the world that he'd been able to take time away from his other cases to support me.

Jennifer launched into her line of questioning, and I answered each one as thoroughly as possible. I focused on Jason, like I was speaking to him as I relayed the events that started it all. Leaving the coffee shop. Waking up in the basement. Then everything that came afterward. I could feel Wainwright's icy gaze on me, but I kept my eyes locked on Jason's.

Jennifer ended her questions, and I felt exhausted emotionally, having relived it over and over again. I was the sole survivor; six other women before me depended on my help today for justice. Jason nodded encouragingly at me as the defense attorney stepped up next. He began his questions, tinged with enough doubt to make the jury reconsider. I watched a dark look flit across Jason's face, and I stumbled. He blinked away his anger and gave me another curt nod. He was here for me. I could do this.

I released a shaky breath as soon as the defense attorney announced his line of questioning was now at rest. Now it was up to the jury to decide how to proceed. We took a brief recess as they deliberated, and Jennifer and I retired to the back room. Nearly two hours later, they had apparently come to some sort of conclusion.

I sat there, my heart in my throat, as one of the members of the jury stood to address the judge. As the guilty verdict went up, a combination of tears and grumbles rose around the court room. I glanced to my left and met Wainwright's gaze head on.

I stood and hugged Jennifer, then greeted my mom and dad as they cheerfully threw their arms around me. I pulled away, my eyes searching the room for Jason's. I met his dark gaze, shooting him a smile and a tiny wave. Before I could do anymore, he was swept away by the crowd and I lost sight of him.

Today had been bittersweet. Though we'd put the man behind bars, this was officially the end of my relationship with Jason. Not that there'd been anything to begin with anyway. But now I had no reason to see him anymore. Over the past year he'd never given me any kind of indication that he wanted anything more. He'd been there for moral support; that was all.

I'd hoped that he would want to continue our relationship from before. I thought he'd been attracted to me once. But that felt like a lifetime ago, and whatever feelings had been blossoming between us had died with my abduction. He'd stopped by to check on me from time to time, but I now realized he'd done so out of obligation.... not desire.

He would move on with his life, keep working. And I would... I wasn't sure what I would do next. I had put off finishing college, and I still got anxious going out at night or in large crowds. But life kept going and the world kept turning, and I had two choices. Either stay stuck in place or move on.

I knew I needed to put all of this behind me and focus on the future, but that was easier said than done.

CHAPTER
THIRTEEN

JASON

I stepped into my apartment, locked the door behind me, and pulled out my phone as I headed for the bedroom. I placed an order with the local pizza place down the block, then decided to hop in the shower while I waited for it be to delivered.

As I stepped beneath the warm spray, I hung my head and waited for the tension to seep from my muscles. I'd been on edge for the past few days, but I wasn't quite sure why.

That was a lie, of course. I knew exactly what was bothering me. Three days ago I'd sat in that courtroom and watched Chloe testify against the man who'd kidnapped her. I hadn't gotten to touch her. Or talk to her. She was out of my life now for good. She had no reason to see me ever again. And it was depressing as hell.

I cursed myself again for not going to her and telling her how I felt. But how could I? She'd been through hell, and I couldn't in good conscience heap any more on her plate. She was safe now, which was all that mattered. If that meant she was relegated to my dreams, then so be it.

And her face filled my thoughts every waking moment. I knew it was crazy, but I couldn't control it. Those bright blue eyes flashed in my mind, sending a stab of regret slicing through my heart and desire spiraling straight to my cock.

I hadn't been with a woman in more than eight months. Though I'd gone on a handful of dates, hooking up with a random woman felt wrong. All I could think of was Chloe. I knew I'd get her out of my mind eventually... But today wasn't that day.

I fisted my erection and stroked hard, gritting my teeth against the delicious pain. God, the things that woman did to me. Over the past year I'd seen her from time to time as she prepared for the trial, and I swore we'd formed a sort of connection. She was like no woman I'd ever known, and I'd wanted time and again to tell her how much I admired her, how much I wanted her. But it was wrong. It would have been a conflict of interest to get involved with her, and now... Now all I had were the memories kept locked away in my heart.

Heat licked over my skin as I slid my hand up and down my shaft, imagining it was her hand on me. Her gorgeous full, pink lips. The thought of her mouth wrapped around my dick, her tongue stroking and flicking over my flesh, was my undoing. I braced one hand on the wall as I came hard, her name a ragged groan on my lips.

I stayed like that for several minutes before finally summoning the energy to wash up. I had just stepped out of the shower when a knock came from the front door. That was quicker than I expected. Wrapping a towel around my waist, I headed out to the living room. Not bothering to look out the peephole, I threw the door open—and froze.

Chloe's bright blue eyes greeted me on the other side. They dropped to my chest, then lower, before jumping up to meet mine again. I couldn't help my body's reaction to her. My groin swelled to the point of pain as her delicious scent wafted up to my nostrils. Even though I'd come mere minutes ago, unrequited desire for the woman standing in front of me made every cell of my body tense.

"Chloe." My voice was harder than I intended when I spoke. "What are you doing here?"

Her mouth dropped open a fraction, then snapped shut. She gave her head a single tiny shake. "I... I'm sorry. I shouldn't have come."

She whirled around before I could say a single word and started to stride away.

"Chloe!" I was lunging for her before I even realized what I was doing and wrapped one hand around her wrist. With a gasp, Chloe yanked herself from my hold. She stumbled under the motion, eyes wide with terror. I froze, wanting to reach for her but knowing it would only make things worse. I stood there, feeling frustrated and impotent.

Chloe had pulled completely into herself the second I'd touched her, and her lungs rose and fell on unsteady breaths as she rested against the wall behind her.

"I'm sorry." It wasn't nearly enough. I never should have grabbed her the way I did, especially not from behind. In retrospect, I saw it clearly. But at the time, all I'd been able to think about was not letting her walk out of my life again. And now I'd probably ruined it.

"I..." What? I knew it was wrong. Christ, I knew it was, but that didn't stop me from spilling the words on my tongue. "Please don't go."

Those giant eyes of hers met mine and she blinked once. Twice. They were no longer filled with fear, and for that I was grateful. Her arms were tightly wrapped around her middle, though, an obvious sign of her nervousness. Not wanting to spook her, I stayed silent and waited for her to open up to me. She had come to me. Why?

As if reading my thoughts, Chloe's gaze skittered away and

her teeth cut into her bottom lip. "I didn't know where else to go."

I couldn't begin to understand what was going through her mind at the moment, but I didn't want to push her one way or the other. Grasping the knot of my towel with one hand, I leaned back against the doorjamb and studied her. "My door is always open."

She gave a little nod but stayed silent, and several seconds passed before I spoke again. "Do you want to come in?"

She looked torn. "I... I don't know."

"Are you really going to make me stand out here like this?"

I lifted a brow her way, and I swore I saw the tiniest twitch of her lips as she repressed a smile. "I suppose not."

I tipped my head toward my apartment. "I ordered some pizza; it should be here in a few minutes."

"Oh, I don't want to interrupt." She shook her head. "I'll just..."

"Chloe." Blue eyes blinked up at me, and I knew I couldn't let her walk away. "Have dinner with me. Please."

CHAPTER
FOURTEEN

CHLOE

I stood in the hallway fighting to draw in a full breath, my heart racing in my chest. This had all seemed like a good idea an hour ago. Now though, I wasn't so sure. I told myself a hundred times on the way over that I would follow through with it.

My psychologist told me the feelings would eventually go away. My anxiety recently had been through the roof, and together we'd devised a plan for me to try something new once a week. I was supposed to do something the old me would have done without a second thought.

Well, this was definitely new. I didn't even really know Jason, yet here I stood outside his apartment. I was literally setting myself up for the exact same situation I escaped a year ago. I should be terrified.

I was nervous. Worried. But not scared. Deep down I knew Jason would never hurt me.

I still couldn't explain what precisely had prompted me to

get into the car and drive over here. Even when I'd entered the lobby when one of the tenants held the door for me, I hadn't really expected to find myself on Jason's doorstep. But now I was here, and I had to decide what to do. Go in or turn back?

I threw a glance at apartment 7B. What I'd thought was just a turn of phrase, he apparently had meant literally. The door stood wide open, waiting for me to make my decision.

He'd never made any untoward move, never came on to me, yet months ago he'd handed me a card with his personal information written on the back in scrawling black ink. *If you ever want to reach me*, he'd said. Had he suspected I was attracted to him and hoped I'd contact him? I was about to find out. Summoning every ounce of courage, I stepped inside.

Jason had changed and was now relaxing on the couch, one foot propped up on the coffee table. For all intents and purposes, he looked completely at ease. But I knew better. The lines around his eyes and mouth were tight with tension, probably worrying over what I was going to do. I slowly closed the door then locked it behind me, cringing inwardly as the metallic click filled the air.

My heart beat faster, and my limbs trembled with nervous energy before I finally forced myself to turn around and face him. The TV played softly in the background, and Jason smiled as I warily ventured closer.

He tipped his head toward the opposite end of the couch. "Make yourself comfortable."

I jumped when the buzzer rang, and Jason threw a small smile my way as he pushed to his feet. "Pizza's here. I'll be right back."

My heart raced as I watched him hit the button to admit the delivery person, wondering not for the first time what the hell I was doing. This was crazy.

Jason grabbed up his wallet from a small side table, then offered the deliveryman a tip before taking the pizza and locking up again. He strode toward me and slid the box onto the coffee table. "What would you like to drink?"

"Whatever you have is fine."

Jason grinned and tipped his head. "Come on."

I rose, wiping my sweaty palms on my jeans, and followed him into the kitchen. His back was to me as he opened a cupboard and pulled down two plates. I couldn't help but notice the way his broad shoulders filled out the plain tee shirt, rippling and dancing under the fabric as he moved.

"Take these, would you?"

I ripped my eyes away, my cheeks flaring hot as he passed me the plates. If he'd caught me staring at him, he didn't say a word. Jason moved toward the fridge and grabbed two bottles of water. "Good?"

I nodded and he snatched two paper towels from the roll before leading the way back to the living room. He set the waters on the table, then flipped open the box. My mouth watered even as my stomach twisted, and I handed a plate to Jason, who loaded it up.

I reached in with shaky fingers and withdrew a slice of the cheesy pizza. Jason relaxed into the cushions and returned his gaze to the TV. I forced myself to chew and swallow, all the while watching him from the corner of my eye. But he never moved. Unlike a lot of other people, Jason didn't scrutinize me. He didn't check on me every two seconds to make sure I was eating, or watching for the smallest sign of an impending breakdown. He was just... there.

I slowly began to relax and we finished off half the pizza in comfortable silence. He didn't interrogate me, didn't watch me like a hawk to see how I was handling being in a locked room with him. I appreciated all of that more than I could say, and it solidified my opinion that Jason really was the good guy he seemed to be.

He left to put the remainder of the pizza in the kitchen, and I pushed to my feet, then drifted toward the window. His apartment overlooked a park, and I stared sightlessly at the lush green trees below.

A hundred emotions rioted inside me, and I felt like a fool for coming here. What the hell was I thinking? He'd been polite, but he didn't seem remotely interested in me, not the way he had that day at the coffee shop last year. My heart twisted and, deep in thought, I didn't hear him when he stepped back into the room.

"You okay?"

I jumped and whirled toward him, my pulse racing in my veins and thundering in my ears. "S-sorry," I stammered, "I didn't hear you."

He smiled gently but didn't move, and I shifted uncomfortably. "I, um… I wanted to thank you."

He gave a little nod. "You're welcome."

"Not for the pizza," I clarified. "I mean, that too, but… for not interrogating me."

His head tipped to one side. "I would never do that."

I was beginning to understand that. "I know," I said softly. "But I always feel weird when I'm out in public. Everyone wants to know what it was like, how I escaped… This was the first time in forever that I felt like I could relax. It was really nice."

The tension was back in his face, and his tone was tight when he spoke. "You shouldn't have to put up with that."

I gave a little shrug. "People are curious. It's…"

"Rude," Jason cut in.

There was that. I nodded. "I'm just so tired of reliving it over and over, you know?"

"I'm sure," he murmured. "I'm glad you decided to eat with me."

Heat flared over my cheeks and I dropped my gaze to the floor.

"Would you be interested in having dinner with me again, for real this time?"

I snapped my eyes up to meet Jason's. "Like... Go out?"

"Or stay in." He shrugged. "Whatever you want is fine with me."

I was momentarily floored. He knew everything that had happened to me, yet he willingly wanted to go out with me? "Are you sure?"

Jason smiled. "I know I'm a year late, but I was hoping I hadn't missed my chance with you."

"No." I shook my head. "I just..." I trailed off, and Jason sobered.

"If you don't want to go on a date with me—"

"No, I do," I stated firmly. "I'm just surprised is all."

Jason's dark eyes stared into mine. "I wanted you a year ago, and I want you now. Nothing will change that."

Heat flared around my heart, but I couldn't shake the nagging sense of unease. It all seemed too good to be true. There were a dozen emotions roiling in my stomach, and I couldn't begin to decipher all of them at the moment. I needed some time to think.

I gestured toward the door. "I'm sure I've taken up enough of your time. I should probably get home."

"I'll walk you out." Jason nodded, then headed toward the door. "I've got a break between cases right now. How about I pick you up tomorrow around seven?"

I smiled. "I'd like that."

I watched as he grabbed his keys, then locked up behind us before leading the way down the stairs. The whole way he stayed half a step ahead, and irritation flared briefly before realization dawned. He wasn't being rude by walking in front of me—he was protecting me.

The sound of his voice jerked me from my thoughts. "Where did you park?"

"Second row." I pointed, and Jason headed that way.

"You don't have to walk me to my car," I said softly. "I'm a big girl."

"I know." He smiled at me. "But I want to."

I used the key fob to unlock the door, then slid into the driver seat. Jason stared down at me, one hand on the door, waiting until I'd started the engine before speaking again. "See you at seven."

"See you then."

Jason closed my door, then stepped back and shoved his hands into his pockets. I shot a little wave his way, then shifted into gear. I risked a glance in my rearview mirror as I pulled out of the lot, and my heart leaped in my chest. Jason stood in the exact same spot, watching as I drove away.

Back at my apartment complex I parked in my space, then glanced around before climbing out of the car. I continued to scan the lot as I made my way toward the building, and I hung back as a man exited. All the while I watched him from beneath my lashes as he moved down the steps and away from me. Once he was gone I let out a little breath and headed inside.

Inside my apartment, I locked the door and slid the three deadbolts into place. I checked all the windows, then hopped into the shower. I soaped up and rinsed off, thinking about tonight and what tomorrow would bring. He'd asked me out when he didn't have to. That meant something, didn't it? I wasn't sure I could give him all of me yet... but I knew he would wait for me, just as he'd promised.

I left the bedroom door open, then climbed into bed. I couldn't stand the thought of being confined, and I felt immeasurably better knowing I had an avenue of escape, as irrational as it seemed. This was my apartment, but Jeffrey Wainwright had stolen my sense of security.

As I lay there in the darkness, though, I realized something. It was slowly coming back. Thoughts of Jason filled my mind as I fell into the first good night of sleep I'd had in more than a year.

CHAPTER
FIFTEEN

JASON

I pulled up to Chloe's apartment complex, my pulse thundering in my veins. What if she'd changed her mind? I killed the engine and palmed my keys, jingling them nervously as I made my way toward the door. I lifted a hand to open it when she stepped out, stealing my breath.

I allowed my gaze to sweep over her from head to toe before meeting her bright blue eyes. "You look gorgeous."

She smiled shyly. "Thanks."

We stood there for several seconds staring at each other. "I thought for sure you'd cancel."

Her head tipped to one side. "Why?"

"I don't know," I admitted. "I just... I thought I'd scared you away yesterday."

"Not at all."

I held out my hand and my pulse kicked up when she placed her fingers trustingly in mine. I tugged her forward. "Would it be weird if I said I missed you?"

"Would it be weird if I said I missed you, too?"

I cracked a grin. "No. I think I like the idea of you missing me."

She didn't say anything, but the shy little smile that curved her mouth and tinged her cheeks pink told me everything I needed to know. I squeezed her hand. "I thought about you a lot last night."

She'd been in my thoughts constantly, more than usual. I'd woken up in the middle of the night so fucking hard I'd had to work one out before I could go back to sleep.

She peered up at me with those liquid blue eyes that threatened to slay me. "Me too."

We had to get the hell out of here before I dragged her inside and begged to touch every inch of her. I gave a gentle tug to her hand. "Come on. I have reservations for us downtown."

I held the door for her as she slid inside, then rounded the car. "Anything you don't eat?" I asked.

"Fish," she replied. "I'm not allergic or anything, I just don't like it."

I nodded. "I'm not a huge fan either."

We made small talk as we drove to the obscure Italian place I'd chosen. I wanted something small and intimate where she wouldn't feel like she was on display. Though she'd told me she didn't care, it mattered to me. I never wanted her to be uncomfortable, especially with me. Inside, I seated myself in the booth across from her.

"Afraid to sit beside me?" she teased.

I could hear the thread of insecurity in her voice, so I leaned forward and took her hand. "I wanted to give you space. Plus, I like sitting over here."

Her brows drew slightly together, and her eyes flooded with confusion. "Why?"

"Because I like looking at you, and I can see you better from over here." Her cheeks flared and satisfaction welled up inside me. "Besides, if I sat next to you," I admitted, "I don't think I could keep my hands off you."

The waiter showed up to take our orders, promising to be back soon with drinks and appetizers. Once he was gone, I set my hand on the table, palm up, prompting her to take it. After a moment, she twined her fingers with mine. "In case I haven't said it recently, I'm really glad you decided to come on a date with me."

Her smile was so soft and sweet it hurt my heart. "I'm glad you asked. Thanks for this."

"My pleasure." Silence fell for a moment, and my gaze flitted around the intimate, dimly lit restaurant before I faced Chloe again. She'd never really explained why she'd shown up out of the blue.

"I was a little surprised you came to see me," I admitted.

She bit her lower lip. "I'm sorry. I know it was unexpected."

"You know I don't mind that." I shook my head. "But I imagine seeing me brought back a bunch of memories you'd probably rather leave behind."

She was silent for so long that my stomach began to twist into knots, and I shifted uncomfortably in the booth. I was just about to tell her not to worry about it and change the subject when she spoke.

"I replay that night in my mind every single day, imagining what I could have done differently." I sensed she wasn't done talking, so I kept my mouth shut and let her gather her thoughts. "I could have asked Sara to stay with me. I could've been more careful. A huge part of me wishes it had never happened."

My heart clenched with sympathy and I lightly squeezed her fingers. "I can understand that."

Those pretty blue eyes lifted to mine. "I'm not sure you do. Because there's this other part of me that thinks it happened for a reason. It's crazy to think that way, I know it is, but I can't help it. Every time something bad happens, people always justify it by saying things happen for a reason, right?"

I nodded at the rhetorical question. It sucked, but I was a firm believer that shitty things just happened. I'd seen way more than my fair share of people doing terrible things, and there was no worldly explanation for them. Sometimes, you could do everything right and it still wouldn't be enough.

Chloe stared at me. "I really like you."

I opened my mouth to return the sentiment, but she shook her head. "It's not some weird case of hero worship or anything. I feel like there was a reason you walked into the coffee shop that morning. There was a reason that you were put into my path. I don't know what it is, and I don't know what will happen between us, if anything. I just…"

She trailed off for a second then licked her lips. "I just wanted to tell you how grateful I am that I had the chance to meet you. Even though this past year has been filled with bad memories and experiences, you were the one bright spot in all of that."

My heart thundered in my chest, and I wondered if she could hear it from where she sat across the table. This woman was killing me with her brutal honesty and openness. "I wish I could take back every bad thing that happened to you," I said sincerely. "But I'm so glad I met you."

We spent the next hour learning one another's preferences —food, music, movies. Everything under the sun. The more I talked with her, the more I liked her. Not that I was surprised by that. I'd known from the first that Chloe was special. Even in the aftermath of her abduction and resulting trial, the inner light that shone from her eyes was still there. It was slightly more wary now… but it was still there. She'd endured hell at the hands of a madman, but she hadn't allowed him to break her.

Not wanting to end the evening too soon, I ordered coffee for us as well as chocolate cake to share. Over dessert I learned that Chloe was working for a manufacturing company in their customer service department. They allowed her the luxury of working from home, and the situation worked perfectly for her. It wasn't in her field of study, but she was happy enough at the moment to receive a consistent paycheck.

When I could drag it out no longer, I tipped my head toward the door. "I think they're trying to close up. Should we head out?"

As if she hadn't realized it before, she tossed a quick look at the servers cleaning and prepping for the following day. Her cheeks pinked with embarrassment before she turned her gaze back to mine. "I didn't even notice."

"Me, either." I waited until she stood, then followed suit. "I was enjoying myself so much I wasn't paying attention to the time."

Chloe tossed a smile over her shoulder at me as I settled my hand on her lower back and guided her toward the front door. Tonight had been absolutely amazing. Chloe was quickly becoming a very important part of my life, and I hoped this was only the first of many nights spent together.

CHAPTER
SIXTEEN

CHLOE

A comfortable silence settled over us as we drove back to my apartment. But by the time we got inside, my body vibrated with nervous energy. Jason had followed me inside and now stood next to the door, watching me warily. He seemed to sense the shift that had occurred within me but didn't know exactly what to do about it, if anything.

I wanted to reassure him, wanted to tell him everything was fine. But it wasn't. Inside, I was a mess. I'd analyzed every minute of our date over and over on the way home, rethinking my responses and wondering if his had been genuine. By the time I walked through the door, I was questioning everything. Mainly, why he wanted to be with me.

"Are you okay?" he ventured cautiously.

He had to think I was a complete nutcase. It'd been a whole year. Why couldn't I move on? I had tried, damn it. I'd gone out on dates, even with just a group of friends. But it was awkward and stilted, and I always felt out of place. I was like an oddity to them, a novelty rather than a person. Most people saw me as the woman who was abducted and held captive last year. Few of them, if any, cared about who I really was. The only person who treated me like they really cared was Jason.

"I don't know what to do," I admitted.

His head tipped slightly to one side in question. "What do you mean?"

"I can't..." I trailed off and tried to put my thoughts into words. "I'm trying so hard just to be normal, but I just... I feel like something's wrong with me."

Jason straightened, those dark brown eyes boring into mine. "There is nothing wrong with you."

I shrugged helplessly. "I'm so tired of people asking me about it. That's always the first thing they ask. Aren't you that girl who escaped? I'm so tired of being that person. I want to be the woman I was before. You want to know why I came to your place yesterday?"

Tears of frustration burned the backs of my eyes, blurring my vision. "I needed someone to talk to. Someone who wouldn't judge me."

"You can come to me anytime," Jason said quietly.

He held out one hand, and I stared at it for several seconds before sliding my palm into his. A flashback of that day at the hospital hit me, the way he'd stared at me like he wanted so badly to touch me but couldn't. Tonight was the first time I'd held someone's hand in more than a year. I didn't know how I felt about it, to be honest. The idea of allowing someone this close to me again made my heart beat faster, both from exhilaration and terror.

I stared up at him. "I don't want to be the broken girl anymore."

His free hand lifted and the backs of his fingers drifted across my cheek before tucking a lock of hair behind my ear. "You're not broken, Chloe. You're the strongest person I know."

His gaze dropped to my lips, and a strange sensation curled through me. For a moment it felt as if everything had slipped away and I was the old Chloe, confident and carefree. But as quickly as it came, the feeling slipped away.

I wanted him to kiss me, but part of me was terrified. Not of Jason—never of Jason. I knew he would never hurt me. I was scared that, if he got too close, things between us would change. I wanted him to see the woman he'd met a year ago and not look at me with pity or awe as everyone else did, but with desire. Passion. Maybe even more.

"I don't know what to do, Chloe." His voice was low and full of something. Desire maybe?

"What do you mean?" I had no idea why I was whispering, only that the situation seemed to call for it.

"I'm trying so damn hard not to touch you right now. All I've thought about for the past year is you, when I could see you again. Hold you. Kiss you. It's been killing me."

I took a tiny step forward. I remembered the way he'd held me after I'd escaped, cradled me in his arms like he could protect me from anything and everything. I wanted to feel that way again. Safe. Secure. Cherished. Protected.

I lifted one hand and laid it on his chest. "You're the only man I've wanted since..." I trailed off before continuing. "You're the only one I trust."

Whisper soft, he placed his hands on my hips. "You're killing me, Chloe."

"Please," I begged. "For me. I want to forget the past and move forward. Please help me."

"God." His eyes closed and his fingers curled into my flesh. "You have no idea..." Those dark brown eyes opened and stared into mine. "I stayed away. I tried so damn hard. Tell me you really want this."

I felt like I was being pulled in two very different directions. All I knew was I didn't want anyone else. No one made me feel the way Jason did. "I don't know," I admitted on a shaky breath. "I just... I want to try. You're the only person who really sees me. That has to mean something, right?"

"I've seen you, Chloe. Believe me. I..." He trailed off, and my body heated at the sparks of lust in his eyes. "I want to kiss you."

It wasn't a question, but he stared at me for several seconds as if seeking approval, and I finally nodded. My breath left my lungs on shallow pants, and Jason stepped forward, eliminating the space between us. He kept his hands on my waist, tight enough that I felt secure but loose enough that I didn't feel trapped.

His head dipped until it was next to mine and I could feel the heat of his breath wafting over my skin as he lightly kissed my cheek. "You're sure, Chloe?"

His mouth was barely an inch from mine, and I turned my head. "Kiss me."

His lips feathered over mine, achingly tender. I closed my eyes at the sensation, loving the way he held me. Memories pressed in, Wainwright's thick arms around me, choking me, and I sucked in a breath as I battled them back.

Jason lifted away and stared at me. "Good?"

My heart kicked up in my chest, and I forced myself to calm. He was gone. It was only Jason and me now. "Again," I demanded.

I focused on each sensation streaming through my body, replacing every memory of Wainwright with Jason's touch, his hands on me, his lips on mine. If my request surprised him, he didn't show it. Instead he lowered his head and dedicated himself to the task of kissing me deeper, more sensually.

Watching Jason as he kissed me kept the memories at bay. I studied his face, let his scent fill my nostrils as I ran my hands over his biceps and shoulders, committing every hardened muscle to memory. The tiny flame of desire in my core roared to life, and liquid heat slid through my veins as I melted against him. I wanted all of him. I needed to feel him, needed him to take all the bad away and make me whole again. "I need you. I want—"

"No." Jason's voice was thick when he pulled away.

I recoiled, the sting of rejection spiraling through my heart.

"You're not some casual fuck." The press of his fingertips against my lower back implored me to listen. I pushed the dark thoughts away and met his gaze. "I've waited a year for this. I can wait another day. A week, a month... whatever it takes. I want you more than anything, but I want to take this slow. You're going to get to know me, to really trust me."

The intent in his dark eyes sent a hot shiver of need down my spine. "Because once I make you mine, Chloe... I won't let you go."

CHAPTER
SEVENTEEN

JASON

I wished I could read her mind. Her bright blue eyes swirled with emotion, none of which I could decipher. I knew she wanted this—and so did I.

But what I said was the truth. I'd known a year ago that she was different. I wanted to know everything about her. What she liked, what she hated, where she saw herself in five years.

"I'm not fucking you," I reiterated, "but I'm not letting you go either."

I slowly slid my hands down to the backs of her thighs, wordlessly showing her my intent. I grasped her bottom and she wrapped her legs around my waist, her arms winding around my shoulders. I carried her to the couch and settled her over my lap.

My erection pressed against the front of my jeans, and she dropped her gaze to where it tented the fabric. Her hands slipped down my chest then lower, over my abdomen until she stroked along my cock.

"Christ, Chloe. You're killing me, baby."

Her eyes widened, almost full of wonder. "You're hard."

"Hell yes," I ground out. I'd come yesterday in the shower, her name on my lips, then again in bed before falling asleep. Now she was splayed over my lap, palming my cock. So much for my good intentions. "I'm always hard for you; you're all I want."

She wiggled her hips, pressing her core closer. "Playing with fire," I managed.

"I know. I just..."

She needed to regain her confidence, and I understood. "I'm not fucking you," I clarified once more as I pulled her farther onto my cock, rubbing her back and forth. "Just feel, sweetheart. Let go and feel how fucking beautiful you are."

Her hips undulated back and forth, and her breaths came fast and low. Her nails cut into my shoulders, and I palmed her breasts. "Come, Chloe. Use my cock to make you come. I want to watch you."

She hissed in a breath as I slid my hands beneath her shirt then skimmed the cups of her bra. I felt like I was on a runaway train, unable to slow it down let alone stop it. Whatever the hell this was between us, it had been a year in the making and we were both spiraling out of control. I was literally hanging on by a thread. My dick ached for her, and I could feel the heat of her core pressing against me as she writhed in my lap.

"That's it..." I gritted my teeth as my cock swelled to the point of pain, ready to burst. "Goddamn it, Chloe. You're so fucking sexy."

I kept talking to her, using my voice as reinforcement, letting her know that she was with me and only me. "I've got you. Let it all go, honey. Come for me."

Her eyes were closed, teeth cutting into her bottom lip, and the sight of her was my undoing. Heat licked over me, and

I knew I was going to come. She needed this too badly, and I couldn't bring myself to tell her to stop. A little wail of pleasure broke free from her lips as her orgasm crashed over her. Mine hit at the same time, and I grabbed her hips, grinding her pelvis against mine as I let go with a feral growl.

Completely spent and sated, Chloe slumped over me, arms wound tightly around my shoulders, face buried in the crook of my neck. Holy fuck. My heart was racing so hard I could barely breathe. I slid my hands up the curve of her hips then around her lower back. I didn't want to push her limits, but I needed to hold her close. I felt like I was flying in a thousand different directions, and I needed the feel of her pressed against me to ground me.

As my arms banded around her back, she stiffened slightly. I turned my head and gently kissed her throat. "I've got you, baby. Let me hold you, just for a second."

Chloe slowly relaxed in my arms, and my heart swelled in my chest. I'd never known it could feel like this. We hadn't even technically had sex and I was already crazy for her. I was so fucking grateful she had come to me last night.

We stayed that way for several minutes until Chloe finally lifted her head and peered down at me. Her cheeks were flushed a soft pink, and she licked her lips before speaking. "I'm sorry."

I refused to regret it. "I'm not." I lifted one hand and cupped her cheek. "I'm glad you came back to me. Trusted me."

I pulled her head down and kissed her lightly. She clambered off my lap and her gaze dropped to my groin—to the wet spot near the pocket of my jeans.

"Yeah." I smiled sheepishly. "That's what you do to me."

Her smile started small, then grew. "I think I like having that power over you."

I chuckled as I stood and pulled her to me. "No doubt you

do, beautiful. You should know that's never happened to me before. I've never lost it over a woman."

Could I have held off? Absolutely. But I needed Chloe to understand that she was the one with all the control. She'd had that stripped from her once, but never again. From now on, she would know that she was in charge of her body, and it was her choice whether to submit.

She tipped her head up so she could see me better as she looped her arms around my neck. "Imagine what I could do with a power like that."

I couldn't help but grin. Her fierce attitude was coming back full force and I loved it. I was so damn proud that she was pushing herself to move on, to not get stuck in the past. I couldn't begin to imagine how much she'd struggled with intimacy. But Chloe was strong; she refused to be a victim, and I admired the hell out of her for that.

"Can I see you again tomorrow?"

She pretended to think about it for a second, then smiled impishly. "You going to make it worth my while?"

"Absolutely." I slid one hand into the thick curtain of hair and tipped her face up to mine. "I need one more kiss."

She melted into me, and the passion on her lips was the sweetest thing I'd ever tasted. Though I wasn't nearly ready to let her go, I forced myself to break the kiss. For a long moment I stared down at her, studying her flushed cheeks and bright eyes, remnants of lust sparkling in the blue depths. I tucked a strand of hair behind her ear, a strange feeling taking up residence in my chest.

As she pulled away, I knew... this woman was going to wreck my world.

CHAPTER
EIGHTEEN

CHLOE

Tomorrow turned out to be nine days later. Jason had been called out to work another case, and he'd been busy for the past week and a half. It was a good thing, I supposed; I didn't want to move too quickly, but I also worried that he had finally found a reason not to date me.

I wondered initially if he'd used work as an excuse to blow me off, and I was pleasantly surprised when he'd called me a little after eleven that first night. Since then he'd called each night before bed, and I could hear the exhaustion weighing down his voice.

It felt awkward at first, but I had to admit I was flattered to know he was thinking about me. I loved talking to him, and though it would've felt strange if it were anyone else, I told him intimate details I'd never shared before. I told him of my childhood, of all my career plans, and of the ordeal with Wainwright last year.

Sometimes he fell asleep while I was talking, but I didn't mind. He told me that he loved hearing my voice right before he fell asleep, and that was the best feeling in the world. It was crazy to have this connection with someone I'd spent so little time with, but I couldn't help the way I felt.

I'd had my weekly appointment with my counselor yesterday, and we'd spoken about dozens of things: work, resuming normalcy in everyday life... Jason. To my surprise, she was incredibly supportive of my relationship with him. She didn't deem it a case of hero worship as I feared she would; instead, she thought he had a unique perception of my situation since he'd been present at the time.

For nearly an hour, I regaled her with stories of Jason's loyalty, of his apparent feelings for me. I explained how we met, how instrumental he'd been in helping me move on from the abduction and everything that had happened in the aftermath. We delved more deeply into my emotions in that one hour than I had in the past year. With the warning to take things slow and listen to my heart, she encouraged me to foster the relationship, promising that we would talk about it more next week.

For some reason, as I stood in front of the bathroom mirror fixing my hair and makeup, I felt unaccountably nervous. Jason promised he had a day off today, and he'd asked to take me on another date. Instead, I'd offered to cook. My stomach flipped when the buzzer sounded from the foyer.

Studying my reflection, I drew in a deep breath then let it out, slow and steady. I felt a tingle running through my veins, butterflies kicking into flight in my stomach. It had been so long since I'd felt like this. Nervous, but excited at the same time. In a way, it was different even than last week.

After our date, things had gotten a little out of control. Not that he seemed to mind. When Jason left, it seemed as if he had to force himself to put one foot in front of the other as he made his way out of my apartment. He wanted me, and I wanted him more than anything. What I had said the other night was true. I was tired of being the victim, tired of feeling repressed. For the first time in a year, I felt like my old self.

I'd never been the type to actively pursue a man, but neither had I downplayed my reaction when I was attracted to someone. This thing between Jason and me was more intense than anything I'd experienced in the past. It was scary but exhilarating at the same time. Mostly exhilarating. There was just something about him that made my brain and body go absolutely haywire.

That kiss... I'd never felt anything like it before. I felt an undefinable connection to him. He understood me in a way that none of my friends did, not even my family. They had all pushed me to forget what had happened and move on. And I'd tried. For the first couple of months after the attack, I resisted going out in public. When I went out now, I constantly kept an eye on my surroundings. I didn't like anyone to get too close to me, which had made dating hard.

Ironically, I didn't have the same reservations about Jason. He understood me. He didn't try to push me or tell me how I should feel. Instead, he listened and validated my concerns. I couldn't tell if that was just because he was trained for these kinds of situations, or if he truly cared about me. The way he'd kissed me last week told me it was the latter.

My heart stuttered rapidly in my chest as I replayed the events of our previous date. I was both disappointed and relieved that we hadn't gone any further. At the time, I'd wanted to. Part of me still did. But the other part of me was scared. Everyone told me how lucky I was that I hadn't been raped or killed like the other girls. But I didn't feel lucky. I still remembered it so vividly sometimes that it felt like just yesterday. I would close my eyes and see him, smell him... It was almost suffocating.

Being with Jason was like a weight had lifted off my shoulders. I didn't have to pretend with him, didn't have to put on a brave face. He'd held me, kissed me, and for the first time in months I felt like I could finally breathe. What was more, almost unbelievably, he seemed to like me. He was attracted to me, but there was something else too.

His words floated back to me. *Once I make you mine, Chloe... I won't let you go.*

His voice had vibrated with promise, and I believed him. He wanted me, and I wanted him. The only thing standing in the way were my memories.

I hit the buzzer to admit Jason, then shook out my hands nervously. Less than two minutes later, there was a knock at the door. I checked the peephole, and my heart lurched in my chest when I saw Jason's handsome profile on the other side. I unlocked the deadbolts, then threw the door open wide. "Hey."

"Hey, yourself."

A sexy smirk tilted his lips as he stepped inside, and I focused my attention on closing and re-latching all the locks before turning to him. Those dark eyes studied me for several seconds before he stepped close, eliminating the distance between us. One huge hand moved to the back of my neck and he dipped his head and brushed his lips over mine.

He pulled back a fraction. "I've been waiting all week to do that."

My worries melted away as heat filled my cheeks and a warm rush of pleasure spread through my chest. "I've been waiting all week for that, too."

CHAPTER
NINETEEN

JASON

I studied Chloe across the table, watching her stiff movements as she gathered up the silverware and stacked it on her plate. Over dinner I'd caught an occasional glimpse of the old Chloe, but she seemed... stressed. Something was off, though I couldn't pinpoint exactly what it was.

When she carried our dishes to the sink, I followed and leaned against the counter next to her. "You okay?"

"Yep."

Her tone was full of forced cheer, and I placed one hand on her arm, stilling her movements. I waited until her gaze met mine before speaking. "You sure?"

She dropped her eyes back to the sink and blew out a little breath. "You're going to think I'm crazy."

"Never." I lightly grasped her chin, then turned her to face me. "Tell me what's bothering you."

"I keep thinking about last week. About..."

Her gaze skittered over my shoulder toward the couch, and suddenly it all made sense. She was thinking about what had transpired between us sexually. Had it been too much, too soon? "Did you enjoy it?"

She licked her lips. "I did. I..." She hesitated, looking defeated. "I feel stupid even saying this."

I shook my head. "Don't ever feel bad telling me what you want."

"That's just it. I want... more." The word came out on a whisper. "I know I should just let it happen naturally, but I feel better talking about it, you know?"

Her expression was heartbreakingly vulnerable, and I gently tugged her into my arms. It must have taken an incredible amount of courage for her to admit that. "I know exactly what you mean."

I took her hand and pulled her toward the bedroom. "Come with me."

She followed along quietly until we'd reached her bed. "You want to stop, just say the word."

I slid my hands over the curve of her hips, loving the way she felt, the way she clung to me. I knew how deeply rooted her fears and insecurities ran, and to see her willing to give herself over to me meant the world. It filled me with pride. Possessiveness. Obsessiveness, because I knew I would never get enough of her.

I still wasn't going to make love to her. No matter how much she begged, I knew she wasn't ready for that yet. Just like last week when she rocked herself to orgasm on my lap, we were going to take things slow, one step at a time. I refused to rush and risk triggering an old memory; she'd been through too much. I meant what I'd said—I would wait weeks, months, even years for her.

Grasping the hem of her shirt, I slowly drew it up her torso. Her stomach contracted as the backs of my fingers brushed along her skin, and her breasts lifted as she inhaled sharply. I pulled the shirt over her head and dropped it to the floor, then grasped her hips again. I kept every move slow and controlled, determined to take my time with her.

Her eyes were closed, mouth parted slightly, and I just had to kiss her. She responded tentatively, opening her mouth to me a little at a time. I swept my tongue over her lips, gently coaxing her to give in and let me take care of her.

Her arms wound around my shoulders, and I slid my hands down to the curve of her ass before lifting her into my arms. I carried her to the bed and lay her in the middle of the mattress. She blinked up at me then and swallowed hard.

"I'm right here, beautiful." I lay next to her and traced her collarbone with one finger. "It's just me."

Keeping my touch light and seductive, I dragged my fingertips down her sternum and continued lower until I'd reached the dip of her belly button. I spanned her waist with my hand, gradually increasing the pressure of my touch. Her chest rose on another deep breath, but she didn't stop me.

Taking that as a good sign, I moved southward until I reached the waistband of her pants. I slowly worked them over her hips and down her legs, leaving her in nothing but a sexy pink bra and a pair of matching panties.

I kissed one hip bone, then the other. Her breath stilled for a second, and I watched as her hands briefly curled into fists before relaxing once more. Returning to the waistband of her panties, I kissed her pale skin, then dipped my fingers beneath the fabric. Keeping one eye on her and using my mouth as coercion, I slowly worked them off until she was finally bared to me.

Christ, she was the most gorgeous thing I'd ever seen. Her body was tense, and I lightly kissed the inside of her thigh, renewing my promise to her that I would go slow. Her scent wafted up to my nostrils, becoming stronger and clearer the closer I got to her. I couldn't wait to taste her, but I somehow managed to clamp down on the reins as desire raged through me.

As I neared her core, her body tensed even more. I slowed, dragging my lips along her silky smooth skin, taking my time tasting and teasing. Carefully, I slid my hands under her hips, lifting her slightly so she was exposed to my view. Her eyes were closed, the muscles of her abdomen and legs rigid. Keeping my gaze locked on her pretty face, I lowered my head and kissed the bud of her entrance.

Her hands slapped down on the comforter, and I paused but didn't relinquish my hold on her. My lips hovered mere millimeters from her core, and I waited, watching as her hands fisted in the comforter. Darting out my tongue, I traced the outer lips before flicking over the tiny bundle of nerves at the center.

Her muscles contracted, quivering with anticipation and need, and I kissed her again. Then again. I continued my slow assault, watching her, feeling every tiny shudder that rocked through her body. Her hips twitched, then jerked as I dipped my tongue inside her, and I knew she was ready.

I slid one hand around and dipped a finger deep inside her. Her back arched, and she let out a little moan that reverberated through my body and straight into my soul. It sent a shockwave of need through me, and I ground my erection into the mattress, every nerve ending on fire for her.

Her hands lifted, then landed on my head. Her fingers curled into my hair, holding me close. She was so responsive, so sinfully sweet. Her reaction was more than I could have hoped for.

Lust coursed through my veins like wildfire, my desire for her unquenchable. I would never get enough of her breathy moans, the way she writhed beneath me. She was everything I'd ever wanted. She might not believe me yet, but she would.

Chloe was mine.

CHAPTER
TWENTY

CHLOE

I woke up next to a wall. A very hard, delicious smelling wall. I stretched my hand, dragging my fingers along Jason's torso as I buried my nose against his chest and breathed deep. Every inch of him was sheer perfection. He was naked from the waist up, and I hadn't been able to summon the energy to get dressed before falling asleep.

He'd unlocked something in me last night, put me at ease in a way no one else ever could. I knew Jason would keep me safe, protect me from anything and everything. My nipples tightened as his legs shifted and the coarse hair brushed my own smooth skin. One hand rested on my hip, and his fingers curled into my flesh.

"Morning."

His voice was deep and raspy, and it rumbled through his chest, sending a faint vibration through me and causing a flare of warmth to shoot straight to my core. My nipples felt tight and needy, and I snuggled closer, pressing my chest to his to alleviate the ache. The old me wouldn't have hesitated to sleep naked, but the new me was too vulnerable.

This was the first time in more than a year that I had slept without clothes, let alone woken up next to someone. Last night I'd fallen asleep wrapped in Jason's arms, enveloped in the warm cocoon of his body heat. Here I felt safe. Content.

He'd seen me at my absolute worst, yet he somehow made me feel beautiful and perfect. He stripped away all of my insecurities with his loving words and soft touch, and his restraint showed his true character. If he'd just wanted sex, he could've taken me to bed a week ago, or even last night. But he'd pumped the brakes, even when I practically begged him to keep going.

Looking back, I could admit it was too soon. I needed the reinforcement, needed to be slowly led back into intimacy. But Jason had held me tight the whole way, caring for me, making sure that I was comfortable and at ease.

And right now, I was closer than ever to giving in. I wanted him, all of him. And not just because of what had happened with Jeffrey Wainwright a year ago, but because I truly liked Jason. It was scary to admit even to myself, but I desired him. I was falling for him despite every rational warning my brain conjured up. I knew he would take care of me. And I was ready. Judging from the thick bulge pressing against my thigh, he was ready, too.

I shifted slightly, testing him to see how he would react. As I had known he would, Jason turned his hips slightly to the side so his erection was no longer poking into my leg. "Sorry, it's a morning thing."

I smiled. "So I can look forward to this every morning?"

Jason paused, and his fingers tensed where they rested on my hip. "I feel like this is a trick question."

I laughed, then tipped my face up to see him better. I

couldn't help but tease him. "Is it me, or is it like this every morning?"

"Always around you, for sure." His voice was deep and gravelly. "But I wake up hard every single morning."

At his admission, my heart plummeted to my toes. I didn't have time to respond before he continued. "I wake up so hard sometimes I have to rub one out before I get out of bed. Because I spend all night dreaming of you and waking up alone."

My breath caught in my chest, and my heart skipped a beat as I stared into his eyes. They were dark with a combination of passion and seriousness, and I knew more than ever that Jason was the man I'd been waiting for. I wanted him—not just for today, but for a long time to come.

"You're not alone now," I murmured.

"No." He gave his head a slow shake, never taking his eyes from mine. "I'm not."

His hand still rested on my hip, and he gently pushed so I was lying on my back. Gaze locked on mine, he slowly moved over top of me, caging me between his muscled forearms. He bowed his head and brushed his lips over mine. I was more than a little embarrassed since I hadn't brushed my teeth yet, but he apparently didn't have the same reservations.

He nipped my lower lip and slid his tongue into the seam of my mouth, silently encouraging me to open for him. Unable to resist, I let him take control as he parted my lips and swept his tongue inside. My hands moved to his biceps, curling into the hard muscle as he made love to my mouth.

Above me he shifted, and I felt his knees move between my thighs, gradually spreading them farther apart. My heart gave a hard thump as adrenaline rushed through my veins. I felt claustrophobic with his huge body suspended over me, and I broke the kiss to draw in a shaky breath.

"You okay?" I managed a tiny nod, and Jason brushed one

thumb over my cheek. "Come here."

Before I could process his words, we were rolling and I found myself suspended over top of him. His thick arousal brushed along my seam, and I bit my lip. In this position, my breasts hung heavily in front of him, and his gaze zeroed in on them. He grasped the globes, kneading gently and rolling my nipples between his fingers. I shifted on his lap, needing more, wanting to feel him inside me.

Jason rolled his hips, sliding the thick ridge of his erection against the bundle of nerves. He teased my core as he played with my nipples, pushing me closer to the edge. "Jason... Please!"

His hands slipped between us to grab the waistband of his boxers, and he hastily shoved the fabric down. "Condom?"

I blinked. I didn't have condoms. I shook my head.

"Wallet." He jerked his head toward the nightstand and I grabbed it up, then extracted the prophylactic from within. Jason ripped the foil with his teeth then rolled it on, eyes on me the whole time.

I watched his hand move over his shaft as he palmed his cock, and I couldn't help but touch him. He was hot and hard, and he hissed in a breath when I ran my fingers over him. "God, Chloe... Game's gonna be over way too soon if you keep that up."

I released him, then shimmied so I was straddled over him. Grasping my hip with one hand, he grabbed the base of his cock with the other and guided it to my opening. "Last chance, sweetheart."

I shook my head. "I want this—I want you."

I tensed as the broad head found my slit then slipped inside. He stretched me, filling me up inch by inch, until his hard length was seated firmly inside me. I drew in a shuddering breath as I gave myself over to him, trusting him with not only my body, but with my heart and soul.

CHAPTER
TWENTY-ONE

JASON

She felt so damn good. Her inner muscles squeezed me tight, tempting me to just let go and come deep inside her. But I was determined to draw this out, to make this as good for her as possible—because if I had any say in the matter, we were going to do this a lot. Over and over, until she realized that she belonged to me.

Her chest rose and fell on rapid pants, and her hands curled into my chest as she fought to balance herself. I wanted her right here where I could see every inch of her. Her full breasts swung gently from side to side, so close I could bury my face between them, kiss those pretty pink nipples. Glancing down, I watched her flesh stretch around my shaft, gripping me tight as she accepted me.

"Fuck, Chloe... You feel so good, baby."

It was killing me to go slow, but I knew she needed this. She needed to be in charge, needed to know she was safe. I wouldn't push her too hard or too fast, no matter how crazy she made me.

Above me, Chloe closed her eyes and bit her lip, reveling in the sensation. A low sound of pleasure reverberated up her throat, and I bit back a smile as she ground herself against me. "There's my girl."

Her hips lifted and lowered jerkily for several seconds before she finally found her rhythm. She was hot and tight and so fucking wet there was no resistance at all as she moved up and down my shaft. Her walls surrounded me like liquid silk, and heat spread throughout my body.

I grasped her bottom and lifted her slightly, then pressed my hips upward and speared myself deep inside her. Chloe let out a little whimper and arched at the sensation. The motion brought her breasts even closer, and I slid my hands up her sides, keeping my touch firm as I spoke to her.

"So beautiful, Chloe. You're so perfect."

I stroked the undersides of the full globes with my thumbs, then upward to the taut pink tips. I kneaded the generous mounds and teased her nipples, rolling them between my fingers until they stood hard and erect. She arched into my touch and her eyes closed, her teeth sinking into her lower lip. I felt her inner walls contract around my cock where I was still buried deep inside her, and I rolled my hips a little.

A growl bubbled up my throat as the motion forced me deeper into her. Her tits swung gently in front of my face as she lifted up and down, and she let out a little hum of pleasure as I caught the tip of one between my lips.

Her ass cheeks filled my palms, and I curled my fingers into her flesh as she rode me. Her core contracted around me, letting me know she was almost there. She was so beautiful when she came; I wanted to see that look on her face again and again.

I thrust roughly upward, pulling her hips toward me at the same time, forcing myself deep until I bumped her G-spot.

Tugging one tight peak between my teeth, I skated one hand up the curve of her waist and tweaked the other.

"Oh, God... I'm—"

Her inner walls constricted, strangling my cock, and I knew she was getting closer. "Let go, beautiful."

I lightly bit down on her nipple as I drove up into her. The mixture of pleasure and pain pushed her over the edge, and she came on a broken cry. Her hips jerked several times as she rode me hard, her orgasm sweeping her away. She curled her hands into the skin of my chest as her entire body tensed, then slumped forward. I caught her weight easily, holding her tight as I continued to pump up into her, drawing out her orgasm as long as possible. Her body shuddered once more, and she let out a little cry. I slowed my strokes, knowing she had to be sensitive.

Her breath wafted over my neck, her chest rising and falling against mine on hard pants as she came down from her haze of pleasure. Turning my head, I kissed her forehead. "That was incredible."

Her head bobbed in what I assumed was a nod, and I rolled us so she was on her back once more. Her arms looped around my shoulders, and I dipped my head to kiss her. She was so damn sweet, so perfect she made my heart ache. I wanted to stay buried inside her forever, but the need to come was almost overwhelming, each second of being surrounded by her silky heat pushing me closer and closer to the edge.

Propped on my elbows, I framed her face with my hands. Chloe's bright blue eyes popped open, and I swore my heart fell right out of my chest. This woman was everything I'd ever wanted—and I wasn't about to let her go.

I started to move, slowly at first, testing the waters. As I pumped my hips, stroking in and out of her tight channel, I trailed my lips over her beautiful face. I kissed her nose, her cheeks, her temples. I didn't think I'd ever wanted a woman this much.

Emotion rose up inside me like a tidal wave, and my dick swelled with my impending release. Staring into those ocean blue eyes, I felt myself spiraling, falling fast and out of control. With a guttural cry, I let go and tipped over the edge.

I stroked in and out twice more before spilling my seed into the condom. My muscles shook with exertion, and I fought to keep myself from sprawling over her. I bowed my head and kissed her neck, loving the way her sweet scent filled my nostrils.

I forced myself to move, then disposed of the condom before coming back to bed. Lifting the sheets, I stretched out next to Chloe and wrapped my arms around her as she snuggled close. It didn't matter that the sun shone brightly outside. There was nowhere I'd rather be than right here.

CHAPTER
TWENTY-TWO

CHLOE

I finished up the last of my work for the day, then logged out of the computer system. I leaned back in my chair and scrubbed my hands over my face.

My job was easy but tedious, and I was beginning to detest it more and more as the days passed. Recently, I'd even considered going back to school to finish my degree, or trying to find a different job more relevant to my intended field. Unfortunately, that would mean having to reenter the work force... in public. I didn't mind going out from time to time, but I was always surrounded by friends or family. I knew I would eventually need to get back out there, but I wasn't sure I was quite ready yet.

My stomach rumbled, and I glanced at the clock in the lower corner of the computer screen. It was well past dinner time, and I pushed from my chair to go in search of food. I grabbed a single-serve frozen entrée from the freezer and popped it into the microwave, then settled back to wait as it cooked. My gaze strayed toward the hallway that led to the bedroom, and warmth settled over my skin.

A different hunger nagged at me, and I picked up my phone, hoping to find a message from Jason. My screen remained infuriatingly blank, and I let out a little sigh. He'd been called out again on another case a week ago, and he seemed to have pulled away.

I wasn't aware of the details of the case—he wasn't able to tell me much—but I sensed it was something bad. He'd called only twice this week before bed, and his voice was full of some emotion I couldn't name. After only a few minutes of conversation, we'd hung up, leaving me feeling needy and insecure.

I hated feeling that way, because I knew it wasn't his fault. His job was incredibly demanding, both physically and mentally, and I knew he was doing his best to juggle everything. Still, the knowledge didn't lessen my disappointment. I only hoped that things would improve once he was back.

I quickly ate, then showered before bed. I kept my phone near me at all times, but it remained quiet all evening. Finally, just when I was about ready to give up on him, the familiar jangle of my ringtone pierced the air. I damn near lunged for my phone and snatched it up, my heart slamming against my ribs when I saw Jason's name.

"Hello?"

"Hey."

Jason sounded weary, and my heart pinched. "How's everything going?"

I knew he wouldn't be able to offer any details about the case, but that wasn't what I was after, anyway. I wanted to know how he was dealing with whatever they had found. "It's... bad," he finally admitted. "Sometimes I just... I hate this."

I heard him swallow hard, and I bit my lip at the pain lacing his words. I felt terrible for doubting him, even for a second. "I'm sorry." I wasn't quite sure what else to say. "Are you making any progress?"

"Yeah." He blew out a breath. "We should be done here soon, but it might take a couple of days to get everything wrapped up."

"Okay." I hesitated a beat when he remained quiet. "I miss you."

"I miss you, too. God, do I miss you." I heard the rustle of something in the background, and I wondered if he was in bed, too, or just getting back to his hotel room for the night. "I can't wait to see you again."

His softly spoken words tempered my disappointment, and I smiled. "I'm all yours. You just tell me when."

"I'll let you know when I'm home," he promised.

"Can't wait."

We said our goodbyes, then hung up. I stared at the phone in my hand for a minute before plugging it in and placing it on the nightstand. I hated being away from him, not being able to share whatever he was going through. He sounded absolutely miserable, and my heart hurt for him. I wished there was something I could do.

For now, all I could do was offer silent support and be there if and when he was ready to talk. I hoped he would get things wrapped up quickly because I missed him like crazy. I tucked one hand under my cheek as I rolled to my side, wishing he was next to me as I finally drifted off to sleep.

CHAPTER
TWENTY-THREE

JASON

I scrubbed my hands over my face and took a deep breath. The past six days had been sheer hell, driven by desperation and fueled by determination.

I fucking hated kid cases. The most recent victim in a series of child abductions and murders, ten-year-old Jade Sommers had been kidnapped from her home a week ago. The screen on her bedroom window had been sliced open, and she'd been taken from her bed in the middle of the night.

We'd apprehended the suspect, but Jade... The damage had been done. She'd made it to the hospital but died just hours later. I would never get the sight of her broken body out of my mind. George Studebaker, a janitor at the mall where Jade's mother worked, had admitted to raping and assaulting Jade, as well as three other young girls over the past eight months.

This was the worst part of my job—seeing the absolute worst of humanity, watching evil walk the earth, completely unrepentant. He'd taken Jade's innocence and ultimately her life. I wanted to tear him apart piece by piece, do to him exactly what he'd done to those little girls.

We'd finally wrapped up the case yesterday, but as much as I missed Chloe, I couldn't bring myself to go to her. My emotions were still too raw; I wasn't in a good place. I'd begged off, promising to take her to dinner tonight instead.

The clock was creeping closer and closer to five o'clock, and I knew I'd have to get ready soon to go pick her up. I needed to get out of the house and forget about work for awhile. Because the longer I sat here dwelling on it, the angrier I became. My job was a huge stressor, and I could feel it putting a strain on my relationship with Chloe. Weeks like the one I'd just had put me in a dark place, and I usually needed several days to recover.

Typically when I felt like this I wanted to push everyone away, retreat into my own head. But this time, I wanted to see Chloe, to surround myself with her goodness and try to push all the bad shit to the back of my mind.

I leaned back in my chair and stared sightlessly at the desktop in front of me. My email sat open, untouched, and I sighed at the list of unread messages. I began to click through them, mostly junk, when one caught my eye. The name sounded familiar, and curiosity got the better of me as I opened it.

Connor Quentin identified himself as a former Marine who was currently assembling people from all branches of the military to form a private security firm. Quentin Security Group was based out of Dallas, Texas and they were currently looking for someone with both combat experience as well as a computer science background. An old friend had apparently passed my name along, and Con wondered if I would be interested in learning more or coming for a visit.

The thought was damn tempting, especially after the past week. Except... Chloe was here, and she meant more to me than anything. I wouldn't give her up. I was flattered that he'd offered, and the job sounded like a dream. I stared at the email for several minutes before finally closing it out without responding. It'd already sat in my inbox for more than a week; no doubt he'd already found someone else.

I pushed from the chair and strode into the bathroom, then flipped on the shower. I turned my mind to Chloe as I stepped under the spray, counting down the minutes until I could see her again.

CHAPTER
TWENTY-FOUR

CHLOE

Dinner was fairly tense. Though I was excited to see Jason after a week apart, I knew something was bothering him. I wondered if it had something to do with the recent case he'd been working. The lines around the edges of his eyes and mouth were tight, his shoulders slumped slightly forward as if the weight of the world rested on them.

Sympathy seized me as I stared across the table at him. I could only imagine how he felt. I had experienced it firsthand when I was kidnapped, but Jason did this day after day, dealing with disappointing blows more often than not. I knew the feeling of not helping the victims weighed heavily on him.

I wished there was something I could say, something I could do to make it better. But I of all people knew how hard it was to accept those words of encouragement. All I could do was stand beside him and silently support him as he sorted out his emotions.

All I wanted to do was go home, show him without words how much he meant to me. "Are you ready?"

Jason offered me a wan smile that didn't reach his eyes. "Sure."

The bill had already been paid, so I grabbed my purse from the chair beside me then slung it over my shoulder and stood. Even distracted, Jason was always attentive to me. He settled one hand on the small of my back and guided me through the maze of tables to the front door. A small crowd of people who'd just entered blocked the front door, and I stood off to the side, waiting for them to disperse before exiting.

An older, heavyset man stared intently at me. I still didn't like the way people paid attention to me, and I flashed him a quick smile before averting my eyes, hoping he wouldn't recognize me. No such luck.

A moment later, he was right in front of me. "You're Chloe Danvers, right?"

"I..." My throat closed up, unable to speak.

He didn't wait for my response as he shoved his phone in my face. "I'm Karl Nelson from the Tribune," he greeted. "How do you feel about the trial? Were you pleased with the outcome?"

I stared blankly at him for several seconds. "I... I guess, yeah."

"Excuse us." Jason's strong, steady voice came from behind me, and his fingers pressed gently into the flesh of my back.

The reporter stepped even closer. "You testified that he tried to sexually assault you, but you fended him off. How did you manage that?"

I'd been trying so hard to put all of that behind me; the last thing I wanted to do was rehash all of those dirty details, especially in front of a dozen other people. I could feel their eyes on me, staring, judging, and my skin flashed hot as my pulse accelerated.

"Don't say a word," Jason spoke low in my ear as he

wrapped an arm around my shoulders. I could hear the thread of tension in his voice, like he was trying desperately to maintain his composure, as he directed his next statement to the group of people milling around. "Excuse us, please."

I quickly scanned the crowd for an opening, but I was trapped. Jason maneuvered me so I was behind him, partially obscuring the view of the group gathered near the doors, but they seemed to surround me, stealing all the oxygen in the room. I felt their gazes on me, curious and penetrating, and I clutched at Jason's shirt.

Undaunted, Karl tried to lean around Jason's broad form. "None of the other women managed to escape. How were you so lucky?"

The question struck me like a dagger. It was the same thing I'd asked myself a thousand times. I had no idea why I'd survived when he could have just as easily raped and killed me as he had the others. I still remembered the smell of the dank cellar, saw the bloodstains on the mattress... Felt Wainwright's hands and mouth crawling over my body.

The floor tipped beneath my feet, and black crept into the edges of my vision. I had to get out of here. *Now.*

My heart raced in my chest, banging against my rib cage with heavy thuds. My breath came faster and faster as he continued to interrogate me.

"How did you...?"

The remainder of his question was lost to me as my thoughts spun out of control. I gasped, trying to drag in breath to no avail. It felt like a vise had clamped down around my lungs. My knees buckled as my vision went black, and I barely registered the sound of angry, raised voices over the blood rushing in my ears. My lungs hyperventilated, and I felt a strong arm band around me, then sweep me off my feet.

"You're okay, sweetheart." Jason's voice barely penetrated

my haze of panic, and I grasped onto it like a buoy in a tempest. "Just breathe, Chloe, I've got you."

After what felt like forever, my vision began to clear and I registered a distinct difference in temperature. I blinked against the glaring light, and I realized I was draped over a bench on the sidewalk, staring into a bright street lamp. I closed my eyes and drew my first full breath in what felt like hours.

"Everything's okay," Jason soothed next to my ear. "I'm right here."

I grabbed for him, and he clutched my hand. "I'm... I'm okay."

"We should get you checked out."

I shook my head, then gradually shifted to face him. The bench was hard and unforgiving, and I grimaced as I rolled to my side.

"Chloe, we—"

"I'm okay." I closed my eyes again for a second before meeting his gaze. "It was just a panic attack. I'll be fine."

"That didn't look fine." His words were harsh, but I knew they were born of concern.

"I know. Thank you for getting me out of there," I said softly.

"That asshole—" Jason abruptly cut off as he threw an angry glare toward the restaurant and the reporter inside.

"Thank you."

Jason redirected his gaze to me, then brushed a kiss over my forehead. "I'm just glad you're okay. Scared the hell out of me."

I released his hand and he helped me into a sitting position.

"You still look pale," he observed. "Are you sure you don't want to go to the hospital?"

"Just home." I took his outstretched hand and stood, then

followed him to the car. Jason drove to my place, then ushered me inside and locked the door. "Do you need anything? Aspirin, Tylenol...?"

I shook my head. "I just want to lie down for a bit."

It was silly, but I felt exhausted as if the panic attack had zapped my strength. I changed and brushed my teeth, then climbed into bed. Jason followed mere minutes later and pulled me in close. Just having him near calmed me, and I slipped off to sleep.

CHAPTER
TWENTY-FIVE

JASON

I knew she was awake. The sun had risen more than an hour ago, and shortly afterward I had felt the telltale shift of her body as she came awake. She hadn't said a word, and neither had I. I continued to lay there quietly, my body wrapped around hers, knowing she needed time to deal with the events of the previous night.

Finally, Chloe scooted toward the edge of the bed. I reluctantly let her go, watching as she moved toward the bathroom. Heart hurting for her, I slipped from under the covers and followed behind as she stepped into the shower and stood listlessly beneath the spray. Once more, I enfolded her in my arms, offering silent support. She tucked her head into my shoulder, and I smoothed my hands down her back.

In my estimation, there were few things that a hot shower couldn't fix, and I grabbed the soap from the shelf then slowly began to lather her body. She stood stock-still under my ministrations as I swept my hands up her arms then down her back, gently massaging the tension from her muscles. Her face tipped up to mine, and I saw the need deep in her blue eyes.

I bowed my head and kissed her, gently at first then more firmly as she wrapped her arms around my shoulders. Time slipped away as I kissed my way over every inch of her, following the little trail of bubbles as they slid in rivulets down her body and circled the drain. I dropped to my knees and slipped my tongue over her navel, then moved lower, to the apex of her thighs.

Her hands fisted in my hair, and I moved between her legs, gently encouraging her to open for me. I drew my tongue through her folds, tightening my grasp on her hips as her muscles trembled. I licked at her, drinking up every drop of her sweetness as I set about trying to make her forget. She pulsed against my tongue as she came on a broken cry, her hands clutching at my shoulders to keep from falling.

I kissed my way back up her body until I claimed her mouth. She kissed me back with no hesitation, tongue sliding against my own. Pushing her gently backward, I braced her against the wall, then lifted her legs, loving the way they automatically wrapped around my waist. The head of my cock slid between the cheeks of her ass, and I shifted her hips so I was pressed against her core. Chloe let out a little whimper as I slid into her on a smooth, deep stroke.

Her walls clenched around me, clasping me tight as I pumped in and out. I made love to her slow and deep, no barriers between us. I should've checked with her, but I knew she was clean and so was I. She told me last week that she was on birth control, and the knowledge was almost disappointing.

I wanted Chloe with a desperation I'd never felt before. I wanted to marry her, wanted to watch her grow round with our children. I wanted her every day for the rest of my life. The timing was fucking terrible, but I couldn't hold my feelings back one more second.

I broke the kiss and stared down at her. Her eyes were closed in ecstasy, teeth buried in her bottom lip as she clung to me.

"Chloe."

Those beautiful blue orbs blinked open and met mine, and in the depths I read every emotion that roiled inside me. Desire. Love. Devotion. My cock swelled as I stroked in and out. "I love you."

Her lips parted, and her eyes went wide with surprise. "I..."

"Shhh." I dipped my head and kissed her into silence. "I just wanted you to know. I will always take care of you. I will always love you."

Her walls contracted around me and her nails bit into my shoulders as she came, flooding my cock with her wet heat. I followed seconds later, pulsing deep inside her body. My legs shook from the effort, and I pulled out of her then lowered her to her feet. Her arms tightened around my neck as she stared up at me.

"I've never told anyone I love them before," she admitted.

"You don't—"

With a shake of her head, she cut me off. "You're the only person who's ever truly seen me, who's ever cared about me. I think I fell for you the second you walked into the coffee shop."

Heat spread through my chest, and I pulled her in for a long kiss. The water eventually turned cold, and I flicked it off before drying both of us. We dressed in companionable silence then headed to the kitchen. Chloe slumped into a chair at the kitchen table, and I studied her. I was worried about her, even though I knew she'd bounce back. All I could do was be here for her, help her through.

"I hate it here," she whispered.

All night long, fury and concern had plagued me. I'd thought about the episode at the restaurant, thought about how I wanted to whisk her away to someplace she'd never have to deal with it again. An idea that had lain dormant for the past couple of days flickered to life.

"Do you really feel that way?" Now that she was thinking with a clear mind, I wanted to know exactly where she stood.

She nodded, looking incredibly forlorn. "I never want to see another reporter as long as I live."

The reporter was an asshole, but so were the supposed friends who'd treated her poorly after the attack. "Chloe." I settled in the chair next to her and turned her slightly so I could see her better. "If you could do anything in the world, what would it be?"

She lifted one shoulder, avoiding my gaze. "I don't know." She sighed. "I'm just tired of being reminded about it constantly."

I could understand that. "Have you ever been to Texas?"

Her blue eyes lifted to mine, and she tipped her head to one side. "Texas?"

I nodded. I knew it was crazy, but the more I thought about it, the more I thought it would be good for both of us. I hated my job, and Connor Quentin's offer was sounding better by the minute. I didn't know if he would still have a spot open, but it was worth a shot.

"There's a job offer in Texas. I never said anything about it before, but if you're open to going and at least checking it out..." I trailed off and she stared at me for nearly a full minute before nodding.

"I think it's worth a try."

I kissed her lightly, then grabbed up my phone and pulled up the email from a couple weeks back. I asked Con if the position was still available and told him that we would be interested in visiting. Less than five minutes later, my phone dinged with an alert, and my heart raced with anticipation as I pulled up his response.

A slow smile spread across my face as I turned to Chloe. "How soon can you pack?"

CHAPTER
TWENTY-SIX

JASON

It didn't take much for Chloe and me to get a long weekend off work, and a week later I found myself in Con's office at Quentin Security.

During the past forty minutes or so, he'd shown me around the facility, and we'd discussed job description, pay, and other expectations. Although the building was still in various phases of renovation, it was all coming together well. I told him about Chloe and her abduction, and the possibility of moving down here for a fresh start.

Con laced his fingers together over his abdomen as he leaned back in the chair. "Blake Lawson just started an assignment at a local healthplex. His charge is a psychologist. I've heard she's very good if Chloe would like to speak with someone."

"I'll pass that on to her, thank you." I jumped right to the heart of the matter. "What do I need to do? Do you have an application for me to fill out?"

He gave an abbreviated shake of his head. "If you want it, the position is yours."

I should've been surprised, but I wasn't. Doubtless, Con knew everything about me before I even stepped foot in the door. I wanted to jump at the opportunity, but I had to make sure Chloe was okay with the change too. We'd spent yesterday exploring Dallas and so far she'd seemed to enjoy it.

"When would I start?"

"As soon as you're available. I've also got another handful of guys lined up to start as soon as they reach the States."

I stood and slipped my hand into his. "I really appreciate this. Can I have 24 hours to think about it, talk it over with Chloe?"

"Absolutely." Con tipped his head. "Take all the time you need."

He escorted me back to the lobby where I found Chloe sitting on the couch. She shot a smile my way and stood as I neared. Con held out a hand to her. "It was nice to meet you, ma'am."

"You, too." Chloe smiled sweetly. "I really admire what you do."

"Thank you. I hope to see more of both of you."

I took Chloe's hand and led her out onto the sidewalk. Once we were settled in the rental car, she turned to me. "What do you think?"

I started the car then turned on the air-conditioning. "I think it's hot as fuck down here."

She let out a tinkling laugh. "It definitely is that."

I sobered as I stared at her. "I really like it. Con is a good guy, and I think he'd be great to work for. I'll primarily be based out of the office so I won't be in the field all the time."

Her big blue eyes studied mine. "Will you miss it? Not being in the field, I mean. Might be hard to go back to a desk job."

I definitely wouldn't miss all the evil and depravity I'd dealt with for the past several years working for the FBI. I shook my head. "I don't think so. This gig seems pretty perfect. The pay is good too, so you wouldn't have to worry about finding a job right away."

She bit her lower lip and was silent for several seconds before speaking. "What about living arrangements?"

I reached over the console and took her hand. "I think you know how I feel about all that, right? I just want you."

She squeezed my fingers. "I'd be lying if I said I hadn't thought about this every waking moment. There are tons of schools down here where I could finish my degree, maybe find a good internship program."

Her words filled me with hope and excitement surged through me. This could be so good for both of us. "Are we doing this?" I asked. "Are we moving?"

A huge grin spread over her face. "I think so."

I cupped the back of her head and pulled her close. "I love you. Thank you for doing this with me."

"I'd go anywhere for you."

With that we headed back to the hotel, where we stayed wrapped in each other's arms for a long time.

EPILOGUE

CHLOE

Two Weeks Later

"I think that's the last of it." Jason carried another stack of precariously balanced boxes into the bedroom. "Take that top one, would you?"

I snatched the small box off the top of the tower before it could fall, then watched as he slid the other boxes of clothes into the corner. The moving truck had been delayed by a whole day, so we'd had a sleepover of sorts on the floor last night. I made sure the bed was one of the first things off the truck today, because my body was still stiff from sleeping on the hard floor.

Unpacking was going to be a long and tedious process, but an exciting one. Jason and I were officially living together. It almost didn't seem real. Everything was happening so quickly, but at the same time it just felt right.

Jason tipped his head toward the box in my hands. "That one's yours."

I turned it over, and my brows drew together as I inspected the intricate carvings. It resembled a jewelry box, but I knew I didn't have anything this nice. I flipped open the lid and gasped. A diamond ring was nestled inside the red velvet-lined interior.

When I finally tore my gaze from the sparkling diamond, I realized that Jason knelt at my feet.

"What do you think?"

"It's beautiful, but..." Oh, my God. Was he serious? "Are you sure?"

He rose to his feet and took my hand in his. "I know it's fast, but... I want you, Chloe. I want to spend every single day with you."

His sincerity tugged at my heart. Yes, it was fast but who cared? I loved him and he loved me. Why wait? "I'd love to."

He pulled me in for a kiss, then extracted the box from my hold. He took the ring from the box and slipped it onto my finger. "As much as I want to marry you right this second, we can push the ceremony out as long as you'd like—within reason," he amended. "No more than a couple of years."

I didn't need years. Hell, I didn't even need a week. The last thing I wanted was some huge service with hundreds of people staring at me. I peered up at him. "How would you feel about a quiet civil ceremony?"

His gaze turned speculative. "Is that what you want? We could elope, go away somewhere."

"All I want is you."

He yanked me against him and his lips crashed against mine in a claiming kiss. He pulled back almost as abruptly and stared down at me. "Is tomorrow too soon?"

I grinned. Hey, if we were going to run, we may as well sprint.

Don't miss the next book in the Quentin Security Series!

Ten years ago, Victoria escaped the man who took her best friend's life. Now he's back—and this time, she won't get away. Turn the page for a sneak peek of Blake and Victoria's story, The Devil You Know!

THE DEVIL YOU KNOW

BEKAH

Ten Years Ago

Sometimes trouble found people; other times they went looking for it. I paid no attention to the shoppers swirling around me as I stared at my best friend. "Are you crazy?"

"What? It's not like they're going to miss them." Leah rolled her eyes as she dangled the earrings from her fingertips, shaking them in my direction. "Come on, I got a pair for both of us."

She held a set out to me, but my feet felt rooted to the floor. They weren't expensive, and I knew that Leah could more than afford them. But it was the adrenaline rush for her, the exhilarating feeling of narrowly escaping trouble. On the heels of the shock gripping me came anger. "You need to take those back."

"And get caught? Are you out of your mind?" She slipped

the earrings she'd lifted from the store back into her purse, igniting my ire.

"Seriously." I grabbed her arm and tried to propel her toward the store. "We're taking them back."

She dug her feet in, pulling against me. "I'm not going back in there."

A low growl welled up my throat and aggravation took over. "You don't have to tell anyone. Just put them back where you found them and we'll leave."

"Don't be dramatic." Leah let out a long-suffering sigh. "They're, like, ten-dollar earrings."

My gaze narrowed. That was exactly the point. I'd never understood why she did stuff like this. Leah had always been the defiant one, pushing boundaries that I abided without question. She'd lost her virginity at fifteen to one of the school's bad boys and rebelled at every turn, from stealing merchandise to smoking pot.

Leah was often in trouble, but her parents always smoothed the way, keeping any infractions off her permanent record. I'd wondered on more than one occasion if Leah was crying out for attention from her parents, but I never said anything to her.

I'd always been the shy one, self-conscious of my petite, curvy figure and mousy brown hair. Leah was popular, outgoing, always comfortable in her own skin, and she exuded confidence to the point of arrogance sometimes. The Wilsons were wealthy, Leah's father being the third-generation owner of a very successful local plastic manufacturer, so her self-importance came honestly.

Leah was kind of a mean girl, but I loved her anyway. We'd been friends forever, and I knew that behind the blonde exterior lay a smart, sweet person, even if Leah didn't let her out nearly as often as she used to. Since we'd been in high school, Leah had lorded her superiority over others, and I sometimes wondered if she kept me around to make herself look better.

Not willing to argue about it anymore, I dragged her toward the exit, and the doors opened with a *whoosh* as we stepped into the warm summer night.

She leaned into me as we rounded the corner of the building. "I wonder if Brock's coming to Angie's party this weekend."

A figure in the shadows caught us both off guard, and Leah let out a high-pitched squeak of surprise. A man stood on the sidewalk, lit from above by the yellow glow of the four-foot-tall letters on the side of the building. My heart jumped into my throat as my eyes swept over him.

Somewhere in his early twenties, his eyes were black as midnight behind his thick glasses, and his sandy blond hair was parted to one side, giving him a serious, bookish demeanor. The most outstanding feature, though, was the abnormal cleft in his upper lip.

Swallowing down my initial fear, I nodded in silent greeting and skirted him as I pulled Leah toward my car.

"Oh, my God!" she exclaimed. "What a creep."

I lightly elbowed her in the side. "Stop it, he can hear you!"

The man lifted a hand our way, and I offered a small smile even as Leah yanked on my arm.

"Um..." His voice stopped me in my tracks just as I grabbed the handle to open the driver's side door. The man's gaze dropped to the pavement as he shifted from foot to foot. "I hate to ask, but um... do you think you could give me a ride?"

"We're busy, sorry," Leah's unrepentant voice cut in before I could even open my mouth. Shooting me a hard look over the roof of the car, Leah made a face before sliding into the passenger seat.

I studied the man. "How did you get here?"

He shrugged uncomfortably, his eyes reluctantly meeting mine. "My friends." He pointed to a car peeling out at the red light on the main road. "They decided to play a joke on me and left me here."

They kind of sounded like assholes, to be honest. "I have a cell phone. Can you call one of them?"

"Thanks, but I don't have their numbers memorized." He dropped his gaze to the ground and shoved his hands in his pockets. "It's no big deal, I can walk. Maybe someone at the truck stop will help me out."

The truck stop was all the way out by the freeway, several miles away, and it was already dark out. Sympathy tugged at my heart. How often did this happen to him? How often did people treat him badly just because of the way he looked?

"Where do you live?"

He glanced up, hope and wariness mingling in his eyes. "Just out of town, near Cherry Ridge."

Cherry Ridge was a fairly upscale rural area, the homes large and placed far apart, surrounded by dense woods flanking the river. He didn't really look like he fit in with the Cherry Ridge crowd, but I tried not to be judgmental. His clothes were cheaply made but clean, a sign that he took care of himself.

The trailer park. Rolling Meadows was out that way, too, a rundown grouping of doublewides spread over a few dozen acres. My heart went out to him. He probably couldn't afford a car, let alone a cell phone. Guilt assailed me.

"Well..." I bit my lip, carefully considering the dilemma. I'd been raised to help people, and he seemed harmless enough. "I guess we can take you."

"Bekah!" Leah screeched from the passenger seat. "Are you crazy?"

"Hold on one second." I held up a finger to the man and

leaned into the car. "He's stranded, Leah. We should help him."

She shook her head. "No way is he getting in this car!"

"Leah." Was she serious right now? "He needs help."

"Not from us!"

It was rare that I ever stood up to Leah, but... I shot the guy a look again. Standing with his shoulders slumped forward dejectedly, he made for a pathetic sight.

"What's your name?"

His gaze darted to mine. "Marcus. My friends call me Marc."

"Hop in, Marc."

"Really?" Hope lit his features, and I smiled.

"Yep, come on."

"Thanks!"

I slid into the driver's seat and shot a look at Leah who glared back at me, arms crossed over her chest.

"This is a terrible idea," she tossed over her shoulder as Marc climbed into the backseat and closed the door with a *thunk*. "I can't believe we're doing this."

I glanced in the rearview mirror and caught Marc's grim expression. Having been on the receiving end of Leah's sharp tongue before, I knew exactly how he felt. I quickly changed the subject.

"Cherry Ridge, right?"

He met my gaze in the mirror. "Yep. Head that way."

Something in his tone made my insides twist. The way he phrased it made me think that my initial assumption was correct. He'd have us drive toward Cherry Ridge, then let him out before we got to the trailer park. Probably a good thing, too. Rolling Meadows wasn't exactly known for its upstanding citizens.

Putting the car into gear, I backed out of the parking spot and pulled into traffic on the main road, then headed toward the truck stop. Passing the ramps for the freeway, I gestured at the road. "How much farther?"

"Just a few miles. There's a road up here to the right. I'll let you know where to turn."

With a nod, I turned my attention back to the road. Streetlights became fewer and farther between, and traffic was almost non-existent at this time of night. Out here in the country, most everyone was probably already bedded down for the night, ready to greet an early dawn and work the land.

"Right up here."

A road came into sight and I flipped on the blinker. Dust clouded the rearview mirror in the red glow of the taillights as the car churned down the bumpy road. Trees flanked us on both sides, blocking the light from the moon, and I glanced around. I hadn't seen any houses out this way yet, not even a light of any sort indicating anyone lived out here. Unease crept into my stomach, sending up a flurry of butterflies.

"How much farther?"

"Not long now."

I took a deep breath and pressed the brake. "I'm sorry, this is all the farther we can go. We're running late, and we really need to get home."

"This is close enough." Marc's voice was suddenly at my shoulder as he leaned forward between the front seats.

"What are you—?" Before I could even blink his hand whipped out, and I froze as the blade of a knife pressed against my throat.

Leah sucked in a gasp as Marc stretched his free arm toward her, shoelaces dangling from his fingers. "Tie her hands to the wheel."

Leah hesitated, and the blade dug deeper into my skin. I cried out in pain and tears welled in my eyes, clouding my vision. "Oh, God, just do what he says, Leah."

Leah's hands trembled as she reluctantly took the

shoestrings and secured my right hand, then the left to the steering wheel. Marc deftly slipped the keys from the ignition, and I heard the soft jangle as they hit the floor somewhere in the back.

In the passenger seat, Leah whimpered. I tested the bonds around my hands, but they were too tight. I didn't have a chance—but Leah did. "Leah, run!"

With one last beseeching glance at me, Leah pushed open the door and sprinted from the car. Marc let out a low curse and slid out behind her, then took off into the darkness. Fueled by terror, I pulled at the bindings. The more I struggled the tighter they became, rubbing my skin raw. Tears coursed down my cheeks as I fought to get free, to no avail.

Oh, God. The silence outside was deafening, and I prayed that Leah had managed to evade him. I had to get the hell out of here before he came back. I did everything I could think of to get someone's attention—screamed at the top of my lungs, pressed my head against the horn. The night air remained quiet and still, devoid of life. My heart rate increased with each minute that ticked by. How long had it been now? Where was he? And was Leah safe?

A loud thump on the window made me scream, and I jumped as Marc threw the door open. The deadly, metallic glint of a knife suspended the breath in my lungs as he slashed at the shoestrings binding me to the steering wheel.

"Come on." He jerked me roughly out of the car, and I stumbled as the rocks slid precariously under her flip flops.

"Where's Leah?"

His grip tightened on my arms, fingers digging into the tender flesh. "Don't worry about her."

His words sent a ripple of terror racing down my spine. I had to find Leah and get away from here. I could barely make out his face, even from just a few inches away, but I could feel his cold gaze on me. A breeze whipped through the trees, parting the branches overhead and allowing the bright light of the moon to spill over us. His face looked demented in the dim light as his deformed mouth curled into a menacing sneer.

My mind spun frantically as I followed beside him, tripping over branches littering the uneven forest floor. Finally he clicked on a flashlight and the ground in front of us glowed yellow in the bright beam of light.

The leaves on the forest floor looked disrupted, and my blood ran cold as my gaze fell over a scrap of fabric. The material was ragged and marred with dark brown stains. I stepped closer to inspect it and froze, my heart tripping in my chest as a logo jumped out at me. Leah had been wearing a shirt with that same distinct alligator logo tonight.

Reluctantly, my gaze followed the trail to a large, pale lump on the ground twenty feet away. A familiar shoe stuck up from the leaves and I stared uncomprehendingly at Leah, her body twisted at an unnatural angle, the same brown stains marring her skin. My eyes fell to the wide, dark gash that split her throat, stretching from ear to ear.

No, no, no...

Bile rose up, burning the back of my throat. Dropping to my knees in the crumbling leaves, I retched until there was nothing left in my stomach. A rough hand bit into the flesh of my arm again, and I pulled against his grasp.

"Get up." Marc dug his fingers in and yanked me to my feet.

Feeling lightheaded and swaying unsteadily, I wiped my mouth with the back of my hand and regarded Marc. Rage welled up inside me. Pulling my arm back, I threw as much force into the punch as I could. His hands flew up to cover his nose, and I placed a well-aimed kick between his thighs. With a muffled shriek of pain followed by a string of curses, he dropped to his knees.

Not wasting a second, I broke free and ran. My feet slid

over the uneven ground, and my lungs burned with exhaustion as I searched the darkness for some sign of life—a house, a road, anything. The reflection of moonlight glinting off of metal came from up ahead as a bridge came into sight, and my heart leaped in my chest. With a burst of energy, I pumped my arms faster, pushing myself to keep going despite the urge to break down and cry. I would *not* think of Leah right now.

Obscured by darkness, I didn't notice the railroad ties until it was too late. My foot caught on the rail and my teeth gnashed together, sending a frisson of pain through my entire body as I sprawled face-first onto the tracks. Shaking off the pain, I scrambled to my feet and dashed forward as the sound of footsteps reached my ears.

Just as I reached the middle of the bridge, a hand closed around my hair and I was yanked back roughly. The motion brought me to a jarring halt, and I fell to my knees with a sharp cry as pain exploded over my scalp.

One hand still fisted in the long strands, Marc dragged me to my feet. "It didn't have to be this way."

Those fathomless black eyes bored into mine, and ice streamed through my veins. I'd invited this monster into the car with us—and now I was going to die at his hands.

Slowly backing me toward the railing of the bridge, he continued to speak. "You want to know about your friend?"

Tears clouded my vision, and I shook my head violently. I wanted to remember Leah vibrantly alive and happy, not cowering in fear before she died.

Despite my denial, Marc leaned in close and continued. "The whore couldn't even make it good. She tried to fight back, scratched my face until I broke her fingers, one by one. It would have been so good with you."

He rubbed his nose along my jaw and I let out a strangled sob. "Please don't do this, please just let me go!"

He shook his head. "I can't do that."

"Please, I..."

"I'm sorry it has to be this way."

He lifted the knife to my throat, the tip of the blade pressing into the soft flesh. His eyes glowed black in the moonlight, and I forced myself to meet his gaze through the blood-spattered lenses of his glasses. *Leah's blood.* My pulse raced and instinct took over as my knee jerked up and connected with his groin. A scream stuck in my throat as he thrust me away from him. The back of my legs hit the railing, and I teetered there for a moment before I lost the battle to stay upright.

Suddenly I felt nothing below me but air. I didn't have time to cry out, didn't see anything flash before my eyes as I plummeted toward the black water of the river below.

Keep reading Blake and Victoria's story, The Devil You Know, now available everywhere!

ALSO BY MORGAN JAMES

QUENTIN SECURITY SERIES

Twisted Devil – Jason and Chloe

The Devil You Know – Blake and Victoria

Devil in the Details – Xander and Lydia

Devil in Disguise – Gavin and Kate

Heart of a Devil – Vince and Jana

Tempting the Devil – Clay and Abby

Devilish Intent – Con and Grace

Quentin Security Box Set One (Books 1-3)

Quentin Security Box Set Two (Books 4-6)

*Each book is a standalone within the series

RESCUE & REDEMPTION SERIES

Friendly Fire – Grayson and Claire

Cruel Vendetta – Drew and Emery

Silent Treatment – Finn and Harper

Reckless Pursuit – Aiden and Izzy

Dangerous Desires – Vaughn and Sienna

Cold Justice – Nick and Eden

Rescue & Redemption Box Set One (books 1-3)

RETRIBUTION SERIES

Unrequited Love – Jack and Mia, Book One

Undeniable Love – Jack and Mia, Book Two

Unbreakable Love – Jack and Mia, Book Three

Pretty Little Lies – Eric and Jules, Book One

Beautiful Deception – Eric and Jules, Book Two

Hidden Truth – John and Josi

Sinful Illusions – Fox and Eva, Book One

Sinful Sacrament – Fox and Eva, Book Two

Retribution Series Box Set 1

Retribution Series Box Set 2

Retribution Series Box Set 3

The Complete Retribution Series

STANDALONES

Death Do Us Part

Escape

BAD BILLIONAIRES

(Radish Exclusive)

Depraved

Ravished

Consumed

ABOUT THE AUTHOR

Morgan James is a USA Today bestselling author of contemporary and romantic suspense novels. She spent most of her childhood with her nose buried in a book, and she loves all things romantic, dark, and dirty. She currently resides in Ohio and is living happily ever after with her own alpha hero and their two kids.

Keep up with Morgan and stay up to date on sales, giveaways, and new releases at authormorganjames.com